Horni-
Culture

Amelia Dax

Cover by Amelia Dax

ISBN: 978-1-990499-22-7

Acknowledgements

To the best people ever, who encouraged me to attempt writing my odd brand of erotica. Especially those who stood at my door, waiting for the 2nd book.

Prickles

I picked through the rubble. The battles were long over, and the harsh winter erased most of the evidence of the zombie hordes who had attacked the last bastions of mankind.

I know it sounds insane, but trust me, it happened.

After a string of ever-increasing global diseases, most of the population was gone. Not just here, everywhere.

I was one of the few that survived unscathed. Well, not entirely unscathed. My scars were internal rather than external, but at least I was still alive.

I walked the perimeter of my field, looking for fresh growth. The few provisions I'd been able to store over winter were long gone and I had to rely on snaring the small critters that sought the warmth of my cabin for food, fearful that one of them could carry a virus that would kill me, or worse.

Compared to my youth, living in a large suburb, this was a solitary and sad existence.

As I scoured for the first tender shoots of edible ferns and weeds, I was struck dumb by what looked like pink, skin covered appendages on thick stalks coming out from the ground.

I staggered back, raising my knife to ward off their attack, only to realize they didn't move. Unsure what the safest course of action was, I nudged one of the oddly shaped flowers with the tip of my knife, and while it remained motionless, it bled a pearly white substance.

There seemed to be no pulse forcing the liquid through the faint veins. It seeped out like sap.

I looked around and froze again. This time at the sight of a hand.

Just a hand. At first it seemed severed at the wrist, but then I realized it was a plant with a green stalk extending below the palm into the earth.

I struck it down.

Lying there on the dirt, it looked helpless.

As I looked around, I realized there were other plants that looked like feet, an elbow and, much to my surprise, a penis.

That one made me take a closer look. It had the same pale pinkish hue to it as the other plants. I carefully poked at it. It seemed to be made up of petals wrapped around each other like lettuce but firmer. Some sort of phallic cabbage?

Curious, I watched them for a while as the sun rose behind me.

The undead horde that attacked the cities had started off like this. Folks killed by that last virus had been buried in massive graves. Bodies heaped on top of each other. Then, just like in the worst horror movies, hands reached from the soil. Dead bodies clamored to rise from the ground, infecting the living until humans were all but wiped out.

But these weren't whole bodies. No sinew or skin attached one part to another. Their positions were all wrong to be a single human. It was as if I'd discovered a scrapyard of body parts made of flowers.

Even though I hadn't believed in religion for years, I had the inexplicable urge to cross myself.

As I watched and waited, I noticed the hand, with its stalk cut in half, had already started to wither. That gave me an idea of what I had to do to protect myself. Just in case this was a new version of undead that would threaten my existence.

I dug up every piece I could find, cut the roots and smashed them under the heel of my boot. Better to have them die than risk letting them grow.

My hand kept hesitating over the penis. I hadn't seen a living man in almost a year and hadn't had sex in nearly two. It seemed a shame to let the well-hung flower die.

I argued with myself, what harm could a lone penis do?

I covered its roots with soil, and then I cleared the debris to allow it to get sunlight.

The logical, survivalist part of my brain scolded me for being so stupid.

The horny, lonely part of me begged for twenty-four hours before pulling the plug on this experiment. "Yeah," I said out loud, as if making a decree. "Let's call this an experiment."

I had an internal argument all the way back to my shelter. Calling myself all sorts of stupid for allowing my good sense to be swayed by a dick. Had I learned nothing in all those years of bad relationships?

But the horny part of me said, "This way you can have the sausage without having to deal with the whole pig. This is the perfect situation."

As I approached the garden near the entry to my dwelling, I had an idea.

I pulled one of the cages used to protect my tomato plants from hungry deer from its post and retraced my steps to the penis plant. I chastised myself with a grin. A year without human interaction and that was the best name my imagination could come up with? Penis Plant?

Dick flower was worse.

Rod-ney was stupid.

I thought about Shaft, but it was too pink to be worthy of that character name.

Every boyfriend I'd ever had turned out to be a prick. So, in their honour, I decided to name my new discovery, Prickles.

And yes, I giggled at the name I'd given my not-so-little experiment.

Life is hard and you have to grab every moment of lightheartedness that comes along.

Yes, I said hard… and come.

My giggle turned into a full-blown laugh.

Blown!

I doubled over and had to wipe the tears from my eyes.

Enough. That serious part of my brain scolded me. This is not the time for jokes.

I'd sobered, mostly, by the time I got back to Prickles. Diligently, I set the cage around it and made sure it was stable. While I didn't expect the plant to grow legs and walk, I'd already seen a foot and hand. I wasn't about to take any chances.

I also put extra barricades against the entryway to my home that night, just in case Mr. Prickles came-a-knocking.

Over the next week, I tended my regular garden and monitored Prickles. I was almost to the point where I could say the name I gave it without giggling. Almost.

It continued to rise from the earth on a single sturdy green stalk.

Good thing. It would have freaked me out had it appeared as if it was growing legs. It still looked harmless enough, which had me debating the pros and cons of putting it in a pot full of soil and bringing it to my regular garden.

It took a few more days before I convinced myself that it would be easier to care for and observe if it was closer to my home. Plus, I really didn't have the time to traipse out to the edge of the field every day.

Survival off grid takes a helluva lot of work and these days, since there isn't a grid left to reattach myself to, maybe I should just call it survival.

Before I could come to a decision, there were three solid days of rain where I did nothing outside except run to the outhouse.

When the weather cleared, I tended to my garden before taking my shovel and the biggest pail I owned out to the edge of the field to uproot Prickles.

I stood in shock to see how well it had grown. Not so much tall but wide. Its pallid flesh had become rosy. Its green stalk was twice as thick as before the rain. Three leaves grew around the base of the cock-like flower where it joined to its stalk. Two bright green round ones on the bottom and one longer one on top.

Its heavy fragrance was musky and sweet.

As I breathed it in, arousal swept through me, settling between my thighs. Even the sensible part of my brain was speechless.

Ignoring my reaction to the plant, I dug around the outside of the cage, careful not to damage its root system. Like the stalk, the roots were sturdy and clung to the earth beneath them. It took me a while, but I finally got them all free and transferred into the pot. I felt good about the chances of my penis plant's survival after I transplanted it into my garden.

Yes, I kept the plant caged. I'm not entirely stupid, or delusional… well, okay. Maybe a bit delu-lu.

When I finished replanting, I touched the tip of the plant with my work-glove covered finger. Fully aware that if the plant was actually dangerous, the issue would most likely be poisonous sap, not a physical attack.

As I stroked along the petals, I swear the plant shifted into my hand. Not a huge movement but as if it was shifting toward the light. Only it wasn't the light it was shifting toward. It was me.

I pulled my hand back and shook it out as if I'd been burned.

The penis head seemed to droop after I let it go.

I watched it for almost an hour. Nothing else happened. It must have been just my overactive imagination.

It had to have been my imagination.

Plants don't just move on their own.

While I chopped wood to cure before winter and milked my two goats, my attention kept drifting to Prickles.

The plant seemed to be doing okay in its new environment. The tip of its head reached toward the sunny sky, even though it seemed to be tilted toward where I was pulling on the goat's teats instead of at the sun itself.

I laughed at myself. Since when did I have such a vivid imagination?

It was bad enough my twat was still in arousal mode after smelling the plant's alluring scent every time my gloves came close to my face. I was going to have to do something about that heavy feeling between my legs or I wouldn't get any sleep tonight.

Luckily, one of the cucumbers from the early crop I'd started was already close to the right size.

I could peel it afterward and have it for supper. Waste not, want not.

My eyes flew back to the penis plant with its sexy mushroomed shaped head.

No, I scolded myself. It was a valuable experiment. Potentially lifesaving.

There were other body parts growing out there beyond my field. I needed to know what would happen to these strange plants as they grew. I couldn't just lop this one off its stalk the first time I got horny.

When the sun lowered in the sky, I grabbed the biggest of my cucumbers and cut it from its vine and then peeled the tip of the blossom end to make it smooth. It had a nice little curve to it I knew would feel fantastic.

The leaves at the base of my penis plant caught my attention. While I'd been harvesting the cucumber, they'd lowered themselves to wrap the floral cock in a protective swaddle. I didn't think much of it. It's not the first time I'd seen a flower close up toward nightfall.

I washed the cucumber as thoroughly as I could under the waterspout from my well, before taking off my clothes and washing the day's grime from my body. Realizing I'd forgotten to bring out fresh clothes, I shrugged. I hadn't seen another human in months. It was a nice evening, no harm in letting myself air dry while I satisfied the simmering hunger I'd felt all day.

Sitting on the top step of my dwelling, I grabbed the cucumber, opened my legs and spread the lips around my opening.

I used my fingers first. Stroking my entrance and clit until they were slick. Then I used the smooth end of the cucumber to circle my tight little bundle of nerves until I needed more. I slid it into my channel an inch.

Still warm from the early summer sun, it felt close enough to a real cock that I moaned as I pushed it between my pussy lips and into my channel.

I eased it in and out slowly, giving the vegetable a chance to get lubricated before I picked up the pace. I dropped my head back and closed my eyes in order to focus on the sensation of its slightly bumpy skin as it slid in and out of my snatch.

I turned it this way and that, making sure its bend was angled just right to make the tip of the cucumber massage my g-spot.

I moaned every time it rubbed.

Keeping my legs open, I drew them up to my chest, curling forward to get the best angle possible as I thrust the cucumber deeper inside my tight cunt. I rubbed my clit with the fingers of my other hand.

The steady simmer I'd been feeling all day made my orgasm that much more intense as I exploded around the vegetable lodged in my twat. I could feel my walls pulse against it as I came.

When the spasms stopped, I pulled the cuke out and tossed it on the porch beside me. As I sat up, Prickles caught my attention.

The leaves had spread wide again and the penis part looked purple.

Curious, I walked into my garden to get a closer look and saw a long drop of sap sliding out from where the petals bundled tightly together at its tip.

I corralled my wayward imagination. Nope. Couldn't happen. Impossible.

I backed away and fled into my cabin with an inexplicable urge to cover my body.

That night, I watched the penis plant through my window. Waiting for it to move again. Even though it was just a plant, I felt it observing me too. The moon had worked its way across the sky before I felt safe enough to go to bed.

I avoided the plant for the next few days. Sure, I watered it with the rest of my garden, but I carefully gave it a wide berth each time I passed.

Silly, I know.

By noon on the fourth day, it had drooped again with its leaves covering its oddly shaped flower. Its rosy, pink colour fading back to the pallid shade it had been when I first discovered it.

I have to say it broke my heart a little. I crouched down by the plant and reached my fingers in between the wire of the cage. "Hey Prickles. I'm sorry, little fella, I just got spooked."

My eyes widened as I watched the leaves open again. Their movement was slow enough that it wasn't easily detected, yet it took only a few minutes for them to unwrap from around the penis shaped flower and for it to tilt upward until it mimicked a fully erect cock. The stalk also seemed to have perked up and was now ramrod straight.

It was the most amazing thing I'd ever seen.

My fingers gripped the cage. Fear warred with a wave of arousal as the nearly thigh high plant shifted toward me as if seeking the sun.

As if I was its sun.

Its tip brushed against my knuckles and my fingers straightened to stroke along its underside. The entire penis part turned a deeper shade of pink, almost purple in response, and a bead of sap appeared at the end. The plant seemed to emit a scent that expanded my senses.

The horny part of my brain took over. I had an irrational urge to impale myself on this floral cock, so strong it silenced any rational protests. I pulled the cage surrounding Prickles from the ground and carefully eased it over the leaves protecting the life-like cock at the end of the stalk.

I hesitated, unsure what to do. If it was a cucumber, I would have just cut it off with my knife, but the stalk looked so sturdy I wondered if it would be strong enough to withstand part of my weight as I impaled myself with it.

I had a fleeting thought about the potential danger from the sap, but it washed away in a wave of longing. I had to have that cock inside me. I threw off my gloves, undid my jeans and shoved them and my underpants to the ground, awkwardly toeing off my work boots to free my legs.

Thankfully, I'd planted Prickles close to the fence. I straddled the plant, leaned forward and grabbed hold of the horizontal plank between the posts. Gently, I took the now fully purple plant with the mushroom head and ran its tip back and forth between my legs. Once I found my balance, I used my other hand to spread my lips to give it better access.

The sap gathered on the plant's tip, mixed with my lubrication. It started to tingle in the best possible way. Heightening the sensitivity of each of my nerve endings as I moved the tip of the flower back and forth and around my clit.

I had to grab a hold of the fence again. The sensation made my knees buckle.

This wasn't going to work I thought in despair.

I was going to fall and risk breaking the plant.

I shifted my feet around the base of the stalk until my back was leaning up against the fence. My butt resting on the cross plank.

It took only moments for the plant to swivel and stretch toward me. It extended the entire length of its stalk to enable the head to reach the slick lips between my open legs.

Once I felt it was close enough, I wrapped my fingers around its length and tugged it toward me. This time I didn't play around. I shifted my hips to allow myself to push the plant's mushroom head into my tight channel.

It surged forward without actually moving. Entering me deeply until I couldn't take any more of its size. Then it began to pulse against my inner walls, as I carefully drew it out and pushed it back in.

Ho-ly Fuck.

I felt my eyes roll back in my head. This was so good.

I braced my hands on the cross plank of the fence and did thrusting squats onto the penis plant.

Its stalk held firm as I pushed against it.

I don't think I'd ever been this wet before, yet I lost no friction. It was like every pleasure receptor was turned up to a thousand. When I thought I would die from bliss, the top leaf folded itself over my clit and curled in, giving me the last bit of pressure and friction my body craved.

My orgasm exploded.

I could feel my channel squeezing the life out of the plant as I rode wave after wave of excruciating pleasure. It took forever for the sensations to lessen and eventually calm.

I was barely able to stand when the head of the penis plant slid from me and drooped slightly before its stalk managed the shift in weight.

The floral penis was shiny and heavily laden with my juices.

I wanted to prop it up or kiss it and make it better. Hell, I wanted to congratulate it on a job well done. But I was barely hanging on to the fence. My legs felt like jello. I had never had an orgasm like that before, self-induced or otherwise.

I sank onto the ground, uncaring if soil got where it shouldn't.

Now that I was eye level with the ravisher of my girly-bits, I could see him in more detail.

Yes, obviously the plant was a 'him'.

The flesh of the fading purple head was marked with veins more in keeping with flower petals. Despite being thrust roughly, deep into my body, its outer layers seemed to be no worse for wear. It looked happy.

Which I know is weird, but it did. The purple had faded to a pretty pink and the leaves, despite still being drenched with my fluid, looked perky.

Its heady smell still surrounded me, only now it was soothing instead of arousing.

This time I gave the head of the plant a kiss and then I touched it to my forehead and smiled. "Thank you." I whispered.

After the first week, I started wondering if I was being ethical. I worried I was mistreating the first piece of humanity I'd seen in over a year.

But the way that big mushroom head seemed to follow me as I worked in the yard, and wept sap from its tip whenever I came near as it shifted closer to me, I had to believe it was consensual.

Worried about consensual sex with a plant? Maybe I had lost my mind. Even so, I'm not sure I could ever go back to a plain old cucumber again. Even a zucchini or eggplant didn't entice me at all.

Over the course of the summer, the penis plant didn't change much. Its stalk stayed green and strong, the leaves grew fuzzy as the end of August approached and we had sex at least once every day. Even in the pouring rain.

But, as the leaves on my big maple started to turn colour and the nights grew colder, I wondered what would become of Prickles. Should I dig him up and bring him inside for the winter? His root system was wide now, and I wasn't sure he'd fit in a pot anymore.

Still pondering my options, I did my daily chores and began to prepare my yard and garden for the coming weather.

The penis plant stayed ever vigilant, gravitating toward me at the end of each day so he could ravage me as only he could.

I was no shy virgin before the cities were destroyed. But I'd never been as completely satisfied as I was by my favourite plant. It worried me toward the middle of September when I noticed the first signs of yellowing on his stalk. Had I let my indecision go too long?

One last time, I vowed. After this, I was going to dig him up and bring him inside to spend the winter. Anything to try to prolong his lifespan.

I ditched my clothes, despite the chill in the air, and positioned myself on the cross-plank of the fence. He had already leaned in and was gently tapping his weight against the puffy lips between my legs by the time I got my hand in position to spread our combined moisture over my clit.

I gasped. He felt rougher today. The extra texture sent frissons of sensation over my sensitive skin. He seemed to swell in my hand as I pushed him inside.

My eyes rolled back in my head. Every nerve ending was on fire as his sap mixed with my wetness, creating an aphrodisiac so powerful I wasn't sure my heart could take the excessive pounding. I wept with joy as I pushed him in and out of my throbbing cunt. Every move set my body on fire in the best possible way. I had never felt such an intense sexual connection to anyone, anything, in my life.

His head swelled further as I rammed him in time after time until I exploded with the most awe-inspiring orgasm that lasted long past the moment when my legs gave out and I slumped to the ground beside his stalk.

My head tilted back against the fence, eyes closed, barely able to catch my breath again. It seemed like hours before I had the strength to look at my lover.

I cried out in dismay.

He was gone. His smooth pinkish surface had burst like a pinata. An explosion of seeds covered his broken stalk, my thighs and the ground around us.

Without care of my nakedness, I found my shirt and frantically gathered as many of his seeds as I could. I'd plant them. I'd keep them inside with me to grow over winter.

What was I going to do without him? The long cold months loomed long and lonely ahead of me.

As I washed up, I salvaged every seed that I could find caught in the creases between my legs. I put some with the other seeds from my garden to plant next spring. Just in case, my hope for a winter indoor version of Prickles didn't come to fruition.

I fell down on my knees in front of my bed that night, begging whatever god was still out there for mercy and compassion. Please let me grow another plant.

Throughout the last of the autumn and into the winter, I searched the woods looking for more of these strange plants. A hand to hold or even a foot. Something to alleviate the bone deep loneliness I was feeling.

I hadn't felt lonely before finding Prickles. I was too intent on simply trying to survive. My cock on a stalk helped me thrive.

I planted some of the seeds in a sturdy pot and watched over them. During December, January and February, while the cold winter winds blew outside, I tended my pots. Watering the seeds to ensure they had the best chance at life.

Then in early March I saw the first hint of green breaking through the soil's surface. As the seedlings grew and stretched toward the sun, I had another realization as I rubbed my hands over my belly.

The seeds in the pot were not the only ones that had taken root from Prickles.

Amelia Dax

Pussy Willow

I was so pissed at my dad. Nothing I ever did was right, even though I did things exactly as he said.

I get it. Life's hard and the world seemed to end without us, but getting mad at me wasn't gonna make anything better.

I kicked a rock along what used to be the road leading into the city. Now it was just a long strip of cracked pavement. It didn't take Mother Nature long to reclaim the space after the humans stopped messing it up.

Dad is still upset at the way things went down.

H1N1 was a scare, and then there was COVID. Then the diseases came so fast we couldn't keep up with the names.

Mom died just before the world went nuts. People started coming back to life and suddenly no one was alive, and no one seemed to be completely dead either.

If Mom re-animated, she didn't come to find us.

I think that's what broke Dad, even though he would have had to kill her, and then she'd still be dead.

Maybe he's sad because he wasn't the one to give her that final peace. Who knew?

What I do know, is he used to be my hero, but now he is impossible to live with.

The only thing that saved us from the throngs of weirdos, I refuse to call them zombies, was winter. Our farm is further up the mountain and when it gets cold, it gets really cold.

Although I'm not sure the life we're living now was worth saving.

Dad hated it when I went off on my own. He didn't understand that sometimes I just had to get away from him.

17

And I wasn't being stupid. Up here on the old road, I could see pretty far. If something came at me, I could escape or fight back. I had my knife and bow with me.

Who knows, while I was out here, maybe I'd be able to get a rabbit or something to have for supper. There weren't many animals around the house anymore. We either ate them or scared them off.

I'd only gone another hundred meters or so when I heard something in the bushes. It sounded too small to be one of those diseased humans that tried to attack us last year. I slowed down and cautiously approached where I heard the noise, notching an arrow in my bow, just in case.

I stepped off the road and peered into the woods. There wasn't much underbrush in this section, so I could see into the clearing just past the trees. It took me a few minutes to figure out what I was looking at. There was a small deer, a buck, half-turned away from me, intently licking a strange pink flower that I had never seen before.

Not wanting to waste the opportunity, I raised my bow and arrow, aimed at the motionless beast, and let my arrow fly.

It caught him just under the front leg directly at his heart, just like dad taught me.

The deer dropped.

Unbelievable. I still couldn't believe it didn't hear me coming.

I approached the body and looked curiously at the flower the deer had been so focused on licking that it had been oblivious to anything else.

The petals were almost as big as my hand. The outer ones curled back, revealing an entrance to a long tube. Nectar dripped down from its depths. Its musky scent drew me closer.

Ignoring the stag at my feet, I brushed my fingers along the outer rim of the petals, and I swear the flower shuddered. Normally I wouldn't touch a strange plant bare-handed, but the buck seemed to be no worse off for lapping at the flower's center.

The petals were strangely firm and felt like the soft skin of a peach.

I brought my damp fingers to my mouth and cautiously licked them. The taste was so sweet, yet had an earthy undertone. It was addicting.

No wonder the deer had been distracted.

I took a step back, fully intending to drag the deer up to the road so I could field dress it before taking it back to our farm. When I glanced up at the flower again, I had to laugh.

From this angle, I realized it looked like a woman's cunt.

I glanced down at the deer and said. "You dirty old dog. No wonder you didn't hear me coming."

It took me a while to drag the buck up to the side of the road. Luckily, it was a young one and only weighed about two-hundred pounds. While I worked on the carcass, my eyes kept straying back to the strange flower.

In my head I started calling it the Pussy Willow, which made me laugh. When I was done, I left the deer on the road and went back to take another look at the plant and to see if there were any others around. I knew I should take it back and show my dad, but I also felt strangely possessive of it.

I stroked my fingers along its outer petals and watched amazed as more nectar leaked from its tubular channel.

I brought my face closer and breathed in deeply, not really surprised when I felt my dick growing in my pants. At 17 it doesn't take much to get me hard. I'd just started having sex when the world imploded. Since then, I jack off at least once a day, just to take the edge off.

Curious and now horny, I held the flower gently and stroked my finger along the inside of the petals. The nectar made its surface slippery and the petals were pretty firm. Their texture felt more like a vegetable instead of a delicate blossom. I tasted the nectar again and my cock grew even bigger, making the well-worn denim of my jeans feel tight.

Even though I knew it was risky, I undid my pants and pulled out my dick.

As soon as my fingers, still slick from the flower's dew, touched my dick, my knees nearly gave out.

Holy Fuck what was that?

I stroked myself, spreading the slick liquid all over my shaft. It tingled in the best way. Making every movement from my hand feel like a dozen. I widened my stance so I wouldn't fall over and braced myself, using my bow as a cane.

It felt so good.

I opened my eyes to see the flower had lowered and stretched out toward me. The entrance to its petal tube hovered only a few centimeters from the tip of my cock. Without thinking, I pushed forward until the flower engulfed me.

This time I stumbled. The sensations were overwhelming. The flower seemed to pulse against my skin. I was afraid to move. I didn't want to destroy the plant.

But it felt like she, the flower, was urging me forward.

I took a tentative step and thrust inside until the outer petals touched my balls.

Holy Fuck.

I eased back a few inches and then gently re-entered the flower's channel.

It felt even better.

I watched the petals for any sign of damage before I pulled out and thrust in again. They were dripping with the nectar, far wetter than when I'd started.

Just like a woman's pussy when it was turned on.

I thrust again and again, my hold on the stem firm and then I gripped it in both hands as I exploded into it. My cum mixing with the flowers juices as it leaked back out the front.

When I pulled out, I saw that the bottom petals had extended. I vaguely remembered feeling like something was massaging my balls.

Those same petals caught my dripping semen and seemed to absorb it into the plant. None of my spunk hit the ground. The flower kept it all.

I was too spent to freak out.

That was the best sex I'd ever had. Sure, Julia had been 19, and the girl definitely knew what she was doing. But she'd just been out fucked by a flower.

I pulled my jeans back up and adjusted myself. Before leaving, I stroked the outer shell of the flower. Amazed that aside from being a shade pinker than it was, there was no sign of damage to the petals.

"I'll be back." I told it before I turned away.

Dad, as expected, was pissed that I'd disappeared, but thrilled when I came home with a deer over my shoulders.

I'd purposefully left its heavy head and antlers behind, so I'd have an excuse to go back to the plant the next day. Gross, but necessary.

Every afternoon over the next few weeks, I found a way to escape from the farm and head back out to the flower. If I was later than usual, I swear she drooped on her stalk until I arrived. Then, as I watched, she rose in slow motion and angled herself toward the front of my pants.

Who am I kidding? My pants were down before I reached the spot where she grew.

She was eager and ready for my dick between her sweet petal lips.

You'll probably think I'm crazy talking about her like she could move on her own, but I tested it to see if she really could. I brought my hips level with her petals, but just out of her reach.

Then, without me moving a muscle, she drifted close enough to swallow the tip of my cock. She could adjust her position within the perimeter allowed by the length of her stem. I wondered if she could pull up roots and walk, then realized if she could, she would have already followed me home.

To be safe, I built a framework to lean against while I fucked her. Most days when we were done my legs felt wobbly. The last thing I wanted was to fall down and squash her by accident.

Seriously, it was the most amazing feeling when I stood still, and she slipped over my dick until she engulfed me whole. It should have felt creepy or weird but it felt like she was sucking my cock while her inner petals were stroking me with several small tongues.

Julia never felt this good.

After a few more minutes, I couldn't take it anymore and I pulled out to start thrusting into the flower's wet interior. After the slow blowjob… suck-job, petal-job, it only took me three more strokes before I came.

The flower seemed to gulp my jizz. It didn't let any of it escape to its outer petals.

Not like Julia, who spat it out because she said it tasted bad.

I stood there with my cock hanging between my legs. Torn between going home before Dad noticed I was gone or waiting a few minutes and do it all over again.

Hearing Dad call my name from up the road made me sigh and pull my pants up from around my ankles. Not thinking, I ran out onto the road directly from the clearing where the plant lived. I jogged up to my dad and tried to act like I hadn't just had my brains fucked out.

"What the hell?" he yelled as he approached.

"I was just looking to see if I could pick up signs of any other deer." I winced. I knew full well that bucks were solitary and didn't roam together and the does were tending to their fawns.

He looked down at the half-eaten debris on the pavement from my kill a couple of weeks ago. He just shook his head and turned back toward our farm.

I followed him. Not trusting that anything else I said wouldn't be just a stupid. Bummed that I didn't have more time with my flower, I glanced over my shoulder toward where my pussy willow had drooped low again, as if she was also sad at my sudden departure.

The next day, Dad kept me close to the house as if he didn't trust me not to run off.

Probably wise.

Still, he couldn't watch me all the time. We had a lot to do to prepare for the coming winter, and not every task required two people.

He strode off to the lower field, leaving me behind to pile wood. I did it in record time and then slipped away in the same direction he'd gone, careful to stick to the brush at the side of the road leading from our place so he couldn't see me.

Once I was past where he was working in the field, I ran as fast as my legs could carry me. I knew I didn't have much time, but I couldn't miss a day and let her down.

She seemed so dejected when I left her alone.

Once in the clearing, I dropped my jeans and barely waited until she'd started her slow journey up to where I could easily enter her. Gently, I raised her on her stem and put my fingers inside her tight channel. I spread her nectar and my pre-com over the head of my cock to lubricate myself as much as possible. I whispered. "I'm sorry." As I plunged into her before I thought she was ready. I tried to be gentle, but her petals stuck a little as I thrust. I pulled out and stroked her more. As horny as I was, I didn't want to harm her.

Eager to make it good for her, I crouched down until my face was level with her opening. I stuck my tongue directly into her channel and curling it to reach as far inside as I could. Hoping to coax out enough lubricant to fuck her.

The sweet scent surrounded me as she rewarded me by coating my tongue.

My cock was still rock hard and ready to go when I stood up again and plunged into her. I tried to be gentle, but the taste of her drove me insane with need. Unlike before, I pounded into her with abandon. Her sturdy stalk

24

withstood the onslaught, and my hands helped hold her in position until I was done.

There was so much cum that it seeped out through the sides. Making me worry that in my haste, I'd damaged her beyond repair.

I kneeled in the soil, jeans still around my ankles as I held the flower gently and caressed the outer petals. I placed several kisses along her entrance. Silently begging for her to be all right.

The lower petals, the ones that massaged my balls when I was deep inside her, slowly cupped my chin as she caressed me back.

In that moment I felt loved. Cared for. Understood.

I hadn't felt like that since my mother died.

Not that I had sex with my mother. Ewww. That's disgusting.

But even though she was a plant, I knew that she had feelings toward me too. She wouldn't have bothered to comfort me otherwise.

I spent longer than I meant to, stroking her stalk and whispering my gratitude into her opening. "I'll be back tomorrow." I promised as I strode away. Careful not to be seen by my father as I passed the field he'd been working in.

He was calling for me when I snuck back, so I pretended I had been sleeping up in the barn's hayloft. He seemed to believe me.

The next day followed the same pattern. Dad went out to work in the field and gave me tasks around the house to keep me occupied.

I quickly did the chores and then set out to spend time with my flower. It wasn't the easiest thing to jog through the trees with a hard-on, but I was getting used to the sensations. They only helped to build my anticipation.

Then one day, close to the end of August, as I approached the clearing, I heard my father grunting so I skidded to a stop before he could see me.

I backtracked so I could come from the other side, where the underbrush grew thicker. Once I could see my dad's back, I crouched down and then laid on my stomach so he wouldn't be able to spot me.

What I saw broke my heart.

The flower. My flower was spilling her nectar for my father.

There was a sheen over the lower half of his face that told me without words he'd already tasted her sweetness. He'd dropped his pants and leaned on the framework I'd built as he stroked his cock, lubricating it with her juices.

And the bitch was leaning toward him.

I watched my father's eyes widen in surprise as she nudged him with her petals.

Tempting him to slide into her depths.

I put my fist in my mouth to keep from crying out. The pain of betrayal pierced me like a knife.

She loved me. I know she did.

So why was she fucking my dad with the same ferocity as she had me?

I watched as she undulated over his cock, now buried between her petals. I watched the wonder on his face as he thrust into her, and she took it.

Enjoyed it.

Did she like him more than me? Did she appreciate his experience?

I'd only been with Julia and one other girl.

Dad was engaged before he met Mom, and he dated a lot in between. He'd told me once that no one made him feel like my mother did.

Did my flower measure up?

Was he just using her to get his rocks off?

Why did she seem to be loving the feel of his cock sliding through her petals? Did she like the way he swivelled his hips?

I just thrust in and out. Did that make me a terrible lover?

My dad thrust for a few strokes and then he backed off, teasing her outer rim with gentle touches from his fingers. He stoked the upper petal and even from this distance, I saw her whole stalk shudder.

Was that her clit?

Had I been such a selfish lover that I didn't think about exploring her and seeing what she liked?

My dad's grunts got louder, and he thrust into her silky channel one last time and threw his head back and hollered toward the sky. "Fuuuck!"

He withdrew from her confines, all the while he continued to stroke her bloom. Tears glistened on his eyelashes as he whispered to my flower. "I will be back, my beauty."

Matching tears glistened in my eyes. I wanted to shout she's not your beauty, she's mine.

I remained in my hiding place until long after my father had left the clearing. I didn't know what to do.

My logical mind tried to tell me that she was just a plant and didn't understand human relationships. Hell, she let me fuck her immediately after being tongued by a buck. But it didn't ease my broken heart.

Eventually, I stood and walked over to where she grew in the field.

She barely shifted in greeting. Her petals were soft and dry. Even though I pushed my finger into her channel, the surface felt stiff and rough.

This made me mad. "Are you tired or just done with me now that you've had my father?" I demanded. I reached out to stroke her, and she recoiled. Or at least that's what it felt like.

I felt out of control, irrational. My anger at her actions made me want to punch something. Destroy something. My eyes landed on the framework I built.

That my father dared to use while he fucked my lover.

I picked it up and threw it toward one of the trees near the edge of the clearing and watched it fall apart with the impact. Dangling limply in the bushes I'd been hiding under. I kicked at the ground near the base of her stalk.

Too close. I heard a crack.

How had I not noticed? Her stalk was turning yellow. Starting to die.

She was leaving me anyway.

Bone deep sorrow fuelled my rage, and I kicked at her stalk again and again until she was laying in the dirt. Her once vibrant petals crushed under my boot.

My anger flew out of me at the sight. I'd killed her. I got down on my knees beside her and picked her up. Her bloom had separated completely from her stalk and lay limply in my hand.

I cried. Sobs so huge I couldn't take a breath as she just lay there. Her petals still, and the thrum of life I'd sensed within her as she engulfed my cock, was gone. I stayed there for an hour, not caring if Dad noticed I was missing or not.

This was his fault. He made her cheat on me. He made me do this to her.

Then I thought back to what my mother used to do. She'd take a cutting from a plant and soak it in water for a few weeks until it grew new roots.

I had to try.

I ran home across the field. Once I reached the barn, I ignored my father's questioning look and took a bucket we used to water our animals and place my flower in the liquid. I set it outside in the sun to give her the best chance of recovery.

Dad looked at me with an odd expression. "Why did you destroy the plant?"

I hung my head, ashamed. "I got mad because she stopped responding to me after she fucked you."

He didn't seem as surprised as I thought he would. "I did that to your mother when we first started dating."

I met his gaze. "You didn't kill Mom."

"No. But I got all up in her face about not wanting me. I was so insecure that I didn't understand that her not wanting sex when I did, had nothing to do with me."

"Oh." Was all I said. All I could say.

"The plant might have been able to go multiple rounds with you earlier in the summer, but it's almost fall. The end of its life span. It may have needed more recovery time."

"So, when I thought she was dejected because I was leaving, she may have been just tired?"

"Yes." He clapped his hand on my shoulder. "After all the shit that's happened over the past couple of years, I guess I've failed to talk to you about how adult relationships work."

"We've been kind of busy trying to survive." I told him.

29

"I'll do better. There is a lot I need to teach you about life, despite what's happened." He laughed. "I once got your mom so pissed off at me, she claimed she wouldn't stay with me if I was the last man on earth. Since we seem to be the only two men left standing, I don't want to take the chance that a woman, assuming we ever find one, will ever get that pissed off at you."

We both looked down at the pail. "If this doesn't work, we can plant her and hope she had matured seeds that will sprout up again next year."

A few days later, Dad and I stood somberly as we buried my pussy willow in the ground. Each of us hoping she'd be a perennial and sprout in the spring to live again.

She didn't.

But early in June, as I walked along the road, I decided to check to see if another plant had grown in her meadow.

I let out a whoop, and rushed home with my news.

My pussy willow was back. This time, instead of just one, there were over a dozen. Their buds filled out and ready to burst open.

Dad and I were about to have a very happy summer.

The Helping Hand

"Father Hamlin said we must go forth and multiply." I told my wife in exasperation. My hand on her thigh.

"Then he can come here and take some of the load from my shoulders so I'm not dead on my feet at the end of the day." She replied.

"I am tired too." I told her. "I toil in the field in the hot summer heat."

"While I tend the chicken and goats, do the laundry in the creek, make bread from scratch, and slave over the wood burning stove in the middle of the day so you can have a hot meal when you come in at lunch. Then you sit and whittle while I clean up our dishes, bring in the laundry from the line and fold it. Plus, on top of my regular tasks, I'm spending hours hunched over in the vegetable garden weeding and repairing the screens the squirrels keep digging up."

"It is the life we've chosen to lead." I told her resolutely. Had we not come to your grandmother's old cottage, we would have died with the hordes.

"You and I did not choose this path." She argued. "Circumstances chose it for us. Last year, there were stores to buy food, and I had electricity to run appliances. I didn't have to toil for hours just to have a piece of toast."

"The land will provide what we need." I told her nobly.

"Well, it needs to give me a helping hand. Maybe then I won't be too tired to satisfy your carnal needs."

"It's not just for my needs. We planned to have a family after we'd been together for a year. It's been nearly two."

"That was before." She laughed. "If you want me to have a baby, you're going to have to learn how to cook on that god-forsaken stove." She rolled over and spread her legs with a sigh.

I quickly pulled her nightdress up over her hips and, being conscious of her fatigue, I concentrated on the slick feel of her as I thrust inside. I'd been thinking about the way her body engulfed me all day, so it didn't take me long to fill her with my seed. As I looked at her to thank her for her cooperation, I was alarmed and to be honest, a little offended to see she'd already fallen asleep.

It was only a few days later that my wife's spirits rose. Maybe it was because I agreed to let her serve leftover meat without stoking the fire to heat it up and a salad, instead of roasted potatoes in the oven. I'd come in before mid-day after our conversation to explain to her how it wasn't that warm in the house only to realize just how intolerable the temperature actually was in our cottage. It was sobering to realize that even in the garden, she'd had no relief from the heat.

I'm sure Father Hamlin would be proud of the way I adjusted and was looking after my wife.

He'd raised me after my parents died. He was the one who suggested I court my wife and warned me that women were fickle creatures who needed a strong hand to guide them.

Even though we've been hidden away for a year, his words echoed in my mind.

Her good mood persisted for several days, which made me curious. She rushed me out the door in the mornings and seemed flushed if I came in from the field early. I wondered if she was working too hard and vowed to help her do more of her chores. I didn't want her to get sick.

To my surprise, she refused my aid and sent me on my way.

So, I feigned going out to the field and doubled back to spy on my wife.

It perplexed me. Her work was still getting done. The heat had risen in recent days, and based on our previous discussions, I'd expected many more complaints from her.

This was our first full summer. We arrived last year in August. The heat was unbearable to us both then, yet today, she was smiling and humming a tune as she walked through the gardens.

Then, to my surprise, she exited through a hole in the fence that I hadn't noticed, nor had she asked me to repair.

Not sure what I should make of her strange behaviour, I followed her into the woods at a discreet distance to ensure I wouldn't be detected. What I saw blew all thought out of my mind.

My modest wife had disrobed and was kneeling with her head bowed in prayer. "Thank you for the gifts you have given me. A roof over my head, food in my stomach, and a loyal husband who does his best to look after me. He told me that the land would provide for our needs, and you have answered my prayer for a helping hand. I go about my duties now with joy in my heart. Blessed am I among women."

With that, my wife rose on her knees and moved forward. The grass was too tall between us, so I couldn't see what she was doing, but she gave a heartfelt sigh and started to rise and fall, moving her hips forward and back. She arched her back and brought her hands to her breasts, weighing them in her palms and stroking her fingers over their peaks. Every few thrusts of her hips, she'd take one of her nipples between her fingers and pinch them slightly. Pulling them away from her body and then releasing them. They popped back, making her smile with the sensation. "Oh." She moaned. Her voice breathy and aroused. "Right there."

She talked as if instructing someone else, even though she was alone.

Her movements increased their pace, and I was shocked to find myself fully erect under the fabric of my trousers. Knowing it was a sin, but unable to stop myself, I released the button and eased the zipper down over my swollen flesh and gripped myself as hard as I could, not knowing whether I was trying to halt my reaction to her moans or release the tension that was building up inside me to a fever pitch.

My hips moved without my permission and my seed spilled over my hands and onto the trampled grass under my feet.

Spent, I leaned against a tree and pulled my shirt over my exposed genitals. I wanted to call her out for her immoral behaviour, but truly mine had been just as shameful.

She still hadn't seen me, so I drifted back into the shadows. She stood, and I realized I'd never seen my wife fully naked before.

I just pulled up her nightdress and performed my marital duty.

She was a vision. Her hair, pulled back in a simple ponytail. Her breasts were high and firm, like the woman in the dirty magazine my brother once showed me. The space between her thighs was so wet it looked slippery.

While I understood it was lubrication, she'd never achieved that with me. Then again, I'd never fondled her breasts or attempted to arouse her. Sex was a marital duty to be performed. Enjoyment had never been a priority, but now, after seeing her act with such abandon, I wanted her to experience that same level of joy with me.

My anger was suddenly fuelled. What had given her such pleasure?

By the time I looked back at her, she'd straightened her clothes and bowed her head again. "Thank you for all that you have provided. Amen." Then, with a smile on her face, my wife went back through the trees, singing the same hymn she used to sing on our way home from church.

What in the devil's hell just happened?

I fixed my pants and strode over to see what my wife had used to debase herself. I staggered back with shock when I saw a human hand rising from the soil with its palm raised to the sky. "What kind of evil is this?" I said to the meadow as I fell to my knees to examine it before I destroyed it.

On closer inspection, I realized it wasn't a hand at all but an oddly shaped flower. The petals closest to the earth shaped like long fingers, with a fleshy hue, and the base of the flower was bulb-like. It had another group of petals forming a tight bud which could easily be mistaken for a thumb. The bud even seemed to be bent slightly in the middle, giving the appearance of a thumb joint.

Still, it must be destroyed.

I stood up, ready to smash my boot and crush its roots when her prayer, with the repetition of the words I spoke to her rushed through my brain. "The land would provide for our needs." And her additional statement. "You have answered my prayer for a helping hand."

35

I lowered my foot. If this was indeed a gift from God, who was I to destroy it?

The flower was rooted to its spot. Immobile. Nable to escape.

I would meditate on its meaning with prayer before deciding its fate.

I walked back past the house through the woods, not wanting to alert my wife to my presence. Although I freely admit to standing behind a tree and watching her move through the garden.

The hymn of praise was still on her lips and her movements quick and light.

It was the first time since we left the city that I'd seen her truly happy. My self-righteous anger was quickly replaced with regret that it wasn't me who caused her joy.

Over the next few days, while my wife's chores were completed in record time, mine were falling behind. I found it difficult to leave her to gather the hay from the fields when I knew she was naked and communing with nature without me.

The hand shaped flower wasn't sentient. It wasn't a demon come to steal our souls. It was an aid to my wife and thus to me as well. In the evenings, she was no longer resistant to my advances.

Perhaps it helped that I had learned a few things about pleasing my wife from her interactions with the plant. To her shock, I took off her nightgown and pressed my kisses to her face, breasts, and body.

Her moans rivalled those that the flower incited as I used my hand to increase her stimulation. Sliding into her well lubricated body was a miracle in itself. The sensations increased tenfold, and my wife rolled toward me, into my arms when we finished, instead of rolling away.

The plant made both of us happier.

I'd come to believe it really was a gift sent from above.

As I watched her leave the meadow a few weeks later, a thought struck me. If this hand shaped flower taught me how to please my wife, could it help me learn other ways to be pleased?

Was this a gift for my wife or for both of us?

Checking to ensure she had gone back to our cottage, I unbuckled and lowered my pants to my ankles and kneeled in front of the plant. Carefully, I stayed within the now well-worn dents on either side of its stalk that my wife had created. I didn't want her to know of my exploration…. Betrayal?

To my surprise, the flower seemed to gravitate toward me as soon as I was near.

Its path was so slow it was almost imperceptible, but suddenly its finger shaped petals touched the underside of my rod and edged toward my balls. The jointed bud folded itself over me as if holding me in a gentle grip.

Without meaning to, I jerked my hips back. Causing a bead of moisture to escape from the tip of the thumb and spread along my skin.

It was as if I'd been electrified.

My shaft spasmed and grew larger and more erect as I slid it slowly back and forth within the flower's grip.

It seemed to pulse around me. Intensifying the feel of my every movement. The fingers along my underside brushed against my testicles until drops of fluid coated my entire length.

I gasped in shock as pleasure ratcheted through me.

Unbidden and unable to stop myself, I ejaculated all over the plant and its stalk. Ashamed, I reached for the hem of my t-shirt to clean my mess when I noticed the plant absorbing my semen.

I stood on shaky legs, not sure what to think of that.

Quickly, I pulled up my pants and left the meadow. I needed to talk to my wife about the plant, but I wasn't sure how to bring it up without telling her I'd been spying on her or that I used the strange flower to pleasure myself.

I worked hard for the afternoon, eager to distract myself from thinking about how I'd acted. I stopped for lunch only because I knew my wife would worry if I didn't come in from the field.

What to say to her? How to approach the subject of the strange flower and how it made me feel.

Father Hamlin would have answers for me. Was it truly a gift or was it a curse, sent to tempt us like Adam and Eve's apple?

My wife knew something was amiss, but aside from a few questioning looks in my direction, she didn't ask. She was distracted too. Yet, from the way she smiled and hummed while taking care of our home, she had no doubts or second thoughts.

Had the plant replaced me in her affections?

Was it a drug?

Day after day we danced this strange dance of secrets and satisfaction.

She'd head to the garden, then sneak off to the meadow, unaware that I followed her to watch.

I gloried in the way she acted without abandon. Unlike me, she seemed to feel no shame in offering herself to the flower. She played with her marvellous breasts, which seemed to grow under her ministrations. She plucked at their peaks and caressed the mounds of flesh as the sap did its magic, and she shuddered in response. Her head thrown back in ecstasy. Then she'd wilt. So limp that it seemed the flower was the only thing holding her upright.

Each day, when she recovered, she kneeled in thanks for the blessings she'd received. She'd often include me in her list of bounty, "Thank you for my husband, and this wonderful fruit you have given me." And then let her voice trail off with an ambiguous item that I assumed was regarding this flower that had become both a saviour and a devil.

After she left, I'd wait until I was sure she was gone and then shamefully lower my trousers and kneel in front of the flower shaped like a hand and let its petal fingers drift over my skin. Dripping its electrifying nectar over my genitals, smearing it over my length with every thrust of my hips. The petals held my girth firmly with every stroke until semen burst from the tip of my erection to water the plant with white globs, which the flower and her leaves absorbed greedily into their depths.

Leaving me breathless, spent and ashamed that I wouldn't be able to resist the flower's temptation and return tomorrow.

I wondered with much trepidation about how our lives were changing because of this plant before I straightened my clothes and headed back out to the fields.

Our well-being benefited from my wife's renewed energy, even in the heat of the sun. But in the dark of night, when my wife turned in my direction to engage in the marriage act, I couldn't perform.

Now it was her turn to complain.

Anxiety plagued me. I knew how the sweet nectar from the plant's fingertips stimulated our senses. How could I compete?

Disappointed and confused, she'd turn away, and I prayed to the heavens for a solution. I loved my wife, and I felt like I was letting her down. All because I thought a flower was usurping my place in her heart.

Still, every morning, I was back at the plant. Letting it cradle my shaft within its firm petals, shifting to help it coat me in its juice until the stimulation drove my eyes back in my head. Every nerve on fire with the sweetest sensations until my release spackled its leaves with white.

Each day, I noticed the stalk yellow a little more as the autumn approached.

What would we do when winter arrived?

Would my wife and I seek solace in each other's arms without admitting to each other what we'd lost? Or would the secret continue to drive us apart?

Father Hamlin told us both during our premarital counselling that communication was vital. While I was to protect my wife, I should also confide in her when I was troubled, so she could soothe me. But how to confide this to her? I had betrayed her and our wedding vows, just as she had done to me.

It wasn't a man that had divided us, but a flower.

I'd thought to cut it down at the stalk and be done with the problem, but I was weak and yielded to the temptation of protecting the most incredible sex I'd ever had.

That my wife had ever had.

September was growing to a close. The fields were almost prepared for the coming winter and my wife had the gardens harvested except for the late vegetables. Our pantry was full and our cold storage overflowing.

Truly, this year we had been blessed.

The brittle yellow continued to encroach on the stalk of the strange flower.

I was torn between visiting it more often and weaning myself, to prepare for when it was gone. I didn't want to be the one to make it snap in half under my thrusts. While knowing that if I did, our problem would be solved.

Well, my problem would be solved.

The plant and its intoxicating nectar didn't seem to bother my wife at all.

Unable to resist, I pretended to head out to the field after our lunch and then crept behind the cottage and ran through the underbrush to the meadow. I hadn't been able to refuse its lure.

It had been as if the strange flower was calling me to it. A siren's song.

I could only hope to be luckier than those sailors and not end up on the rocks. Damaged beyond repair.

I settled over the petals, my rod firmly in their grip. I could feel their edges had roughened in the afternoon sun. With dismay, I realized we were close to the end.

The plant was dying.

Tenderly, I stroked the outside of the flower. Whispering words of thanks and asking for forgiveness. For what I wasn't sure, I just needed the plant to know I was sorry.

The sensation from the plant's nectar felt weaker than it had earlier that morning. I was soaked yet the electrifying tingle of it along my skin was lacking. I felt a tear slip from my eye as I gently thrust against the dying petals. I closed my eyes, and I opened my other senses to better experience every bit of feeling from what I somehow knew would be our last time together.

My orgasm was softer, gentler, a tender good-bye.

When I'd regained control, I opened my eyes again. Shocked to see my naked wife kneeling in front of me.

She placed her hand over mine as we gently held the flower.

"Love me." She told me. Her voice firmer with command than I'd ever heard her. "This miracle flower has done what was needed. It's time for us to let it go." She tugged on my hand and pulled me with her as she fell backward onto the ground.

With my shaft still soaked with the flower's nectar, I covered her with my body and entered her with an urgency I'd never felt before. Not even on our wedding night.

She responded to me with the same wildness as she had with the flower. She met my body each time I entered her, urging me to match her intensity. Her channel felt slick against my skin, electric as I slid in and out. She gasped each time I entered her and groaned when I adjusted my angle to drive in deeper. She pulled my face toward hers and kissed me in a way that made my soul rejoice.

I thought I'd loved my wife before. It was nothing compared to what I felt for her now.

Overcome with need, I pushed into her with a ferocity I'd never felt before. When my release came, I howled into the air like an animal, then collapsed over her body, barely able to roll to the side so she didn't have to bear my entire weight while I recovered.

"I have watched you." She finally said. "You are not as sneaky as you think you are."

I was too tired to feel the shame trying to bubble up from deep within my mind. "You were suddenly happy. When I found out why, I was both furious and intrigued. I had to see for myself its effects. Then I was ashamed."

"I saw you struggling. I wanted to relieve your worries, but knew you weren't ready to talk. So, I waited."

She paused. "This morning I knew we didn't have much time left. The frost was coming, and the flower was fading fast."

"I felt it calling to me this afternoon."

"I prayed for help. You needed to be guided back to me."

I rolled onto my back, bringing her with me to rest, splayed over my body. "Thank you."

We lay like that under the afternoon sun until it disappeared past the treetops. The shadows grew, even though it was only mid-afternoon. As we stood and dusted the leaves and twigs from each other's skin, my wife gave a dismayed gasp.

I looked to where she pointed and saw that in our passionate embrace, we'd knocked over the stalk and crushed the flower beneath our legs as we made love.

"It did what it came to do." I whispered as I held her close. It didn't bother me that we were still unclothed in the middle of a meadow. It seemed fitting for our return to Eden.

"The land will provide everything we need." She told me. Echoing back those words I'd spoken to her before her discovery of the flower.

"You prayed for a helping hand."

"God definitely moves in mysterious ways." Her smile still held a secret. "It seems, He has also granted one of your deepest desires as well."

I looked at my wife. Completely confused. She knew I wished we had better marital relations. That gift had already been given a hundred times better than I could ever have imagined. Then my eyes widened.

"A child?"

"I think so. I should have had my cycle several weeks ago."

I picked her up and swung her around, uncaring that I was trampling the remains of the flower even further into the dirt.

Playing Footsies

Sometimes you just happen to be in the right place at the right time. Dumb luck is the only reason I'm still alive.

Up until last year, I lived in the city. I had my own podiatry practice and was engaged to an amazing woman.

We'd sold our condos and bought a new home to start our lives together. Our wedding had been only a month away, when it was time for my annual solo-retreat up into the mountains. I'd been doing it since I graduated university.

My uncle had a hunting cabin, which he rented out in the fall. He got me to go there the weekend before hunting season started, to do any repairs and ensure all the summer stuff was put away or winterized. Then he got me to stock the pantry shelves because the hunting season clientele were a different breed.

Instead of families wanting to get away from the city, they just wanted a place to crash, drink beer and play cards.

I'd already talked to my uncle about canceling since the wedding was so close and there was still so much to do.

My fiancée told me she'd just have a girls 'weekend with her friends while I was gone. She'd insisted that if we didn't do things on our own, then we'd run out of things to talk about when we were together.

It was a rule her parents lived by. Since they were still married and acted like best friends after being together for almost forty years, who was I to argue?

I had no frame of reference for a healthy relationship. My parents split before I was a toddler and still bickered every time they saw each other. My uncle never even dated.

When I left for my uncle's place a year ago, it was the last time I saw my fiancée. Now, I was alone with only the belongings I'd packed for that weekend away.

The world went mad after I left, and populations across the globe ceased to exist within weeks.

My fiancée called me on my phone just as I was packing my car to return to the city. She begged me to stay away.

I'd been so busy with the list of tasks my uncle had for me, I hadn't been paying attention. At her panicked words, I realized I'd been smelling a strange acrid scent. I ran into the two-story cabin and raced to the front windows.

From here I could see over the valley to the city beyond.

Huge plumes of black smoke hung like a dense curtain, blocking the skyscrapers from view.

She told me she'd try to find a way to get to me. Her "I love you." at the end of the call was the last time I heard her voice.

After we hung up, I was determined to find her. I went into the small village at the base of the mountain to see if I could find out more about what was going on. The few people I'd seen were busy packing and driving away. Each one of them told me to find some place safe and hunker down. Most seemed irate that I stopped them to talk and cause them further delay.

Unbelievably, they claimed to have seen reanimated corpses walking around.

I thought them foolish and delusional in their panic as I prepared to continue down the mountain to find my fiancé.

That was until I was getting back into my car, and saw an oddly hunched person picking its way across the street.

The stench of its rotting flesh carried toward me on the wind overpowered my senses. I slid into my car and slumped down so it couldn't see me as it passed.

I sat motionless in shock, until it stumbled out of sight.

That night, I replayed in my head every zombie apocalypse movie I'd ever seen. My mind spun, filled with ways to fortify my uncle's cabin and remain undetected by scavengers and what ever the hell that thing was.

The winter was harsh. Luckily, my great-uncle had me stock the cabin in preparation for a full schedule of autumn rentals.

Not that anyone else showed up.

I'd packed my clothes for a late fall weekend in the mountains, so I'd had some winter clothes with me. Still, it had been a fifty-fifty crap shoot for most of January and February to see if I'd survive until spring.

The cabin was well insulated and had a wood burning stove. I'd blackened the windows to keep the light from acting as a beacon to both the living and the 'undead'.

I still thought labelling what I saw as a zombie was unrealistic, but I wasn't about to take any chances and find out for sure.

In the spring. I set out to explore the area. Despite my rationing, the tins of food had run out midway through March and I'd been surviving on whatever I could hunt or catch since then.

Thank God Mom enrolled me in a survivalist summer camp when I was thirteen.

After watching the news, I'd become anxious and obsessed with the world ending. Sending me to a survivalist summer camp was the only thing she'd found that could calm my fears.

Who knew I could see into the future, eh?

As I walked down the slope from the cabin, I took a path that would take me to a grove of maple trees.

The cabin was nestled among spruce and fir. I'd been boiling their needles for tea and snipping the new growth to chew, just to help ward off hunger pangs. But while they were edible, I can't say they actually tasted good.

I hoped the maple would be better. Even though it was late in the season, I hoped I could tap a few of the trees for sap. Anything to give me something new to eat. I'm sure I'd lost at least ten pounds since the canned food ran out.

The only thing that saved me was my uncle's bow and arrow. He had guns too, but I didn't want the sound to carry and alert anyone, or anything, to my existence.

Nevertheless, I carried both today. Just to be safe.

I kept vigilant. I could only assume I'd been safe because of the harsh winter. This side of the mountain was warming quickly. If anything survived the cold, I could be in its path, especially the further I ventured from the cabin.

Ahead, I saw the path widen into a small clearing with the maple trees on the other side.

Still cautious, I slowed my steps to ensure I didn't startle anything that could be in the meadow. I wanted to be able to see them first instead of the other way around.

The sun came through the clouds just as I was close enough to see into the main part of the small field. I bit my lip to keep my surprise silent. There were several human feet sticking up from the ground. Their pale pink looked like healthy skin, and the entire area gave off this alluring scent.

A complete opposite to the diseased creature I'd seen last fall.

Curious, I stepped forward and scanned the rest of the area for anything dangerous before entering the sweet-smelling clearing.

To my surprise and relief, I discovered they weren't real feet. They were plants with foot-shaped petals perched on sturdy, dark green stalks that bore an uncanny resemblance to legs.

There were a few flowers shaped like hands growing among them as well, but they didn't interest me nearly as much as the foot-like plants that grew nearly waist high.

They looked so real. The main flower had a long graceful arch with tiny delicate buds along the angled tip that resembled long, slender toes. Their pale pinkish colour almost matched the shade of my fiancée's delicate skin.

The thought gave me a stiffy.

I was a podiatrist because I had a thing for feet. The smell, the strength in their contours, the delicate toes.

Fuck, just the thought of them made me hard.

Needless to say, my lab coat was always buttoned when I was with a patient.

My fiancé had been into foot play. It made her the perfect match for me.

It's actually how we met. I'd been out with friends at a bar and her feet caught my eye. Occupational hazard, even without my slight little kink. I watched her slender foot drop her sandal to the floor. My drink paused halfway to my mouth as my eyes followed her foot's path as her arch hugged her date's calf as it slid up his leg.

I could practically feel my pant leg shift under her caress. I couldn't take my eyes off the under-table action.

As she lifted her beautifully manicured toes to massage the outside of his thigh, he brushed her away. Her foot dropped to the footrest when he harshly told her to stop it.

Meanwhile, I was as hard as a rock and totally ignoring my friends, who were teasing me as they saw where my attention had gone.

Her date turned back to the people they were sitting with, leaving her to look dejected.

I double checked to see no ring on her finger. When I saw it was bare, I decided to take a chance. In a bold move that was out of character for me, I strode over to where she and her group were sitting at a high-top table. I leaned in close. "I think your feet are exquisite. I would never have stopped you."

She came home with me that night. Six months later, I asked her to marry me.

I had to assume she was dead since I never heard from her after her frantic call. But, looking over the field of feet-like flowers, I felt like she was with me again. I traced my hand along the delicate looking but surprisingly sturdy petals.

At my touch, the fragrance increased.

Its heady aroma acting like an aphrodisiac.

My cock was rock hard in my pants.

To my surprise, the flower seemed to point its toes to the sky as the stalk seemed to move slowly toward me. At first, I thought it was swaying in the breeze, but it didn't flow back and forth. It seemed to deliberately bend toward me.

I knew I should step back and observe from a safe distance, but the fragrance lulled me into a calm. Instead of retreating, I stepped forward until the heel of the firm petals nudged my balls and my cock rested in the arch of the flower. I swear I could feel it pulse against me, even through the heavy denim of my jeans.

I cradled the flower in my hand, ever so slightly pushing it tighter against me, surprised when the petal edges seeped a pearly liquid. Curious, I swiped at the nectar with my finger, and brought it to my nose.

It had a sweet, musky scent to it that made a shiver go through my entire body and settle at the base of my cock. I almost came on the spot.

I felt out of control.

Unable to stop myself, I undid my jeans and shoved them to the ground. I'd stopped wearing my boxer briefs ages ago because they were such a pain in the ass to keep washed.

I gently pressed the flower against my bare skin and rubbed the arch of it over my throbbing shaft. My eyes rolled back in my head and my knees buckled as the moisture spread over my skin. I'd never felt anything like it as I moved the flower head faster until I couldn't hold back.

Huge dollops of cum shot out from my cock and coated the leaves growing out from the plant's base.

To my amazement, instead of sliding off to the ground, the plant absorbed my ejaculate.

Sightly ashamed of my carelessness, I looked around to make sure I hadn't put myself in danger by being so focused on the petal foot that I'd ignored my surroundings.

All was quiet.

My grunts as I orgasmed seemed to have scared off even the small birds in the trees.

Quickly, I pulled up my jeans.

I'd never been a quiet man in bed, and I would be foolish to stay here and risk alerting anyone who might be nearby to my presence. Glancing down at the plant, I knew I couldn't leave it behind. I wanted to explore its aphrodisiac properties. I glanced around and counted the foot-flowers, pedi-petals... I'd have to come up with a better name for them. There were over a dozen, so I took a chance and tried to pull the plant up by the root.

It didn't budge. Which wasn't surprising, given the width of the stalk's base.

Reluctantly, I grabbed my knife and cut off the flower as close to the ground as I could. I felt like I was harming a friend, but I couldn't stay here any longer. Maybe I'd come back tomorrow with a shovel and see if I could transplant some of these amazing flowers.

Damn, I should have thought of that before I cut this one.

Paranoid about being caught at a disadvantage after letting my guard down, I whispered an apology to the damaged plant and caught myself waving goodbye to the others as I left the meadow.

All the way home, I held the flower gently up against my nose so I wouldn't lose its amazing scent.

As soon as I got back to my great-uncle's hunting cabin, I guess it's mine now, I hauled out one of the old five-gallon metal buckets I'd used to melt snow in over the winter. It was the only thing I had with a wide enough mouth to accommodate the huge leg sized stalk. Once it was safely in the bucket, the flower was at thigh height.

I set it on the floor in front of the couch where the afternoon sun was brightest and added a few crushed aspirin to the water. I remembered Mom used to do that whenever she brought roses in from her garden. Somehow, it made me feel better to be giving the plant a painkiller since I chopped it from its roots.

Maybe I was finally going insane after being alone all winter.

The flower didn't seem to be any worse for wear. Its petals still wound tightly over its surface, with no signs of drying or decay around its edges. This made me feel better as I stroked it, trailing my fingers over the top, and teased the creases between what must be buds, even though they resembled toes.

To my amazement, the toe-like growths spread out and flexed beneath my touch. They moved so slowly, like a flower blooming in the morning sun's rays. Had I not been paying attention, I might have missed it.

Once again, my fingers felt nectar secreting from under the petals.

In the close confines of my living room, the scent was almost overpowering.

My cock, which hadn't completely gone down during my walk back to the cabin, was fully erect again.

This time, I didn't hesitate to take off my jeans and sit with the plant was between my legs. I reached out to take some of the nectar dripping from the petal's tips and spread it over my skin. Trying to keep my strokes slow to make it last, but it was as if my hand had a mind of its own. I held the arch of the flower against my cock with both hands. The fresh nectar that seeped out was slick, increasing my arousal to where I feared my sac would explode if I didn't cum soon. The sensation was so intense I had to close my eyes. I leaned back against the couch cushions and held on for dear life.

It might have been my hands doing the work, but I was no longer in control.

I was edging myself.

Every time I felt the pressure in my balls to let loose, my hands loosened their grip. No longer obeying my body's demands to finish the job.

When one of my hands finally dropped away, it was replaced by another sensation. I opened my eye a crack. Then stared in amazement as I watched the foot-shaped flower slowly position itself to raise-the-roof.

It had been one of my fiancée's favourite things to do to me whenever we were out at a fancy restaurant. She'd slide her foot up my inner thigh and point her toes so she could take my cock, which was hard the instant she touched my leg, in the space between her big toe and the rest of her foot and jerk me off.

I'd never believed in reincarnation until now.

I fell back against the cushions and gave myself over to the rollercoaster of euphoria as the flower continued for what seemed like hours to arouse me until I was close to the peak and then ease off again.

If I didn't cum soon, I was going to black out.

As if sensing how close I was to my physical limit, this time when the petals slid along their nectar's slickness, the motion remained steady. Its arch pulsated along my length while its toes wrapped around my tip.

I thrust up into its hold and erupted.

My growled scream echoed in the room as jizz shot out from my cock and coated the flower with thick white cream.

The flower drooped on its stem and lay on my thigh by the time I had enough strength to open my eyes again.

To my shock, the afternoon had already darkened to night.

My walk had been just after midday. I'd returned home with the flower around two. It was now after six. I smiled and said to the flower, already standing straight in its container. "Four hours." I laughed, wondering if I was insane after all, and imagined the whole thing.

Until I spotted the last of my cum disappearing into the plant's stalk. "What a way to lose track of time."

As I prepared something to eat, more fir tips because I'd been so enthralled about the foot-flowers that I'd completely forgotten my initial task of gathering maple buds, I started talking to the plant. It was the closest thing to a companion I'd had since I arrived last fall.

I told it about meeting my fiancée and how she loved to have me play with her feet almost as much as I loved playing with them.

In my imagination, it seemed like the flower understood every word I said.

After chewing on a few twigs until they were just strands of fibre, I laid down on the couch to sleep. I'd blocked off the upstairs rooms at the beginning of winter to keep as much heat as possible in this part of the house. I pulled the blanket up over me and looked at the flower in the firelight. "Good night." I told it. "Maybe tomorrow I'll dig up two of your sisters. One foot is good, two would be even better."

Then I passed out from sheer exhaustion.

The next morning, I could smell the intoxicating fragrance of my sexy foot-shaped flower before I opened my eyes. Somehow it had intensified overnight making my usual morning wood stand twice as tall, thick and eager to come. Keeping my eyes closed, I stroked myself and thought of the way the flower had seemed to bend its petals to satisfy me.

It had been one helluva dream because there was no way it could be true.

I fondled myself, fully immersed in the fantasy of a plant, shaped like a foot and coming to life just to satisfy me. Hell, sometimes I enjoyed my fiancée's foot play so much that having to fuck her almost felt anticlimactic.

I smiled to myself as I kept my hand on my cock, enjoying the feel of the open air.

Then something nudged my hand.

My eyes flew open.

I bolted to stand on the other side of the room and nearly shit myself.

There, bending low on its long, thick stalk, was my foot-flower… flowers?!

Overnight, it had grown a second stem that twisted around the stalk and faced the first one, sole to sole. Both flowers had lowered enough to brush my hand as I stroked myself. Had I stayed in the same position, they could have fucked me between their arches.

I tugged at my hair. Was I fuckin insane?

I glanced over at the plant, half expecting it to pick up its bucket and walk toward me like some B-rated horror movie.

It didn't, but the stems of the flowers straightened, forming an almost perfect o-shape between the petals that had my dick straining toward it.

Flashes from my dream, or what I thought was a dream, had my cock at full mast.

The flower, if it could, looked dejected at my rejection.

I took a deep breath, and the scent soothed me. What if it hadn't been a dream?

Cautiously, I walked back toward the flowers. I reached out to touch the petals and immediately the scent increased and the same milky nectar from my dream coated my fingers. My hand gripped my cock, spreading the silky liquid before my brain could tell it to stop.

Was I having an out-of-body experience?

The sensation lit my body on fire.

I thrust into my fist until it wasn't enough. Without thinking, I stepped toward the plant, which had already turned toward me, so the gap between the flowers was directly in line with the tip of my mushroom shaped head. I plunged in and growled. The pleasure was so intense it was almost agony. I drew out and plunged in again. My hands stroking the tops of the feet and flexing the toe-shaped buds to tighten the arch and increase the friction on my pistoning shaft.

I threw my head back and let out a feral scream as I came. My semen arc'd across the room, leaving a trail of white over the hardwood floor of the cabin.

Fully spent, my knees bent, and I flopped back onto to the couch wondering what the hell just happened.

I swear the plant's flowers, separated at the top yet kept its heels together so it looked like a gigantic smile.

I just sat there and stared at this wondrous plant. Then, wanting to understand as much as I could about it, I stood up to get a better look and discovered that not only had it grown a second flower overnight, it had also grown a root system that curled around itself, half filling the bucket.

This gave me an incredible idea.

After a morning digging up and prepping the soil with some fertilizer I'd found in the storage shed, I planted my new flower in the spot where my great-uncle's second wife had grown a vegetable garden. Then I made the hike back down to the meadow where I'd found the plant and dug up as many of them as I could carry.

Back and forth I went over the next few days until I'd transported all the foot-flowers and a few of the ones that looked like hands, because… well, why not?

They took to their new spots with their roots growing deep and healthy.

I planted other vegetables as well. My uncle had a bunch of seeds. God only knew how old they were, but most seemed to at least sprout in the soil.

As I tended my vegetable garden, I stopped wearing my jeans.

Every time I bent over or crouched down to weed, my foot flowers seemed incapable of leaving me alone and my pants ended up in the dirt anyway.

On lazy summer afternoons, I'd pull out the lounge chair and set it up between the rows of my favourite plants and watch as the feet and occasional hand brushed against my body, spreading their satiny nectar over my skin and bringing me to the brink of orgasm, edging me until I was ready to black out before they took pity on me and let me cum. Then they'd shield me from the afternoon sun, so my skin didn't burn while I recovered.

As fall approached, I gathered as many buckets as I could and cut the newest foot flowers off at the stalk and brought them inside to spend the winter with me. At least I hoped they'd survive.

I lined them up on my coffee table and dragged the kitchen table over as well to crowd as many plants as possible in the window's light.

Of course, I left room enough to walk between them to receive their ministrations and, in return, give them the gift of my seed. Which seemed to feed them better than any other fertilizer.

Maybe I was nuts.

Maybe I died during that first winter and this was just the energy of my soul dreaming of what my perfect life would be. Surrounded by feet. Petal-soft, and incredibly pliant yet firm as they engulfed my cock and made me come again and again for the rest of eternity.

Or I'm just one lucky son of a bitch to experience a never-ending supply of foot-jobs.

Amelia Dax

Ass-ter

It was like a scene from The Walking Dead. The horde pushing against our vehicle, trying to get inside.

To get us.

My husband stomped on the gas, but our SUV didn't move.

Glass broke. Incomprehensible screams echoed through the interior.

Hands grabbed at my husband with their putrid flesh hanging off the bones.

My scream woke me up. Rapid breath, perspiration running down my cheeks, or was it tears?

"You okay?" a stranger's voice asked.

Reality chased the last of my dream away. I recognized the voice of my saviour. "Yeah. It was just another bad dream."

"They will eventually go away." He reassured me.

"Really?" My chuckle held no mirth. "It's been over five months. I think they're going to stick around for a while."

"You don't get over shit like that in a day." He rolled over. "It's early yet. Try to go back to sleep."

"No, thank you", I thought to myself. Sleep was the last place I wanted to be. They weren't just dreams. They were the last images I had of my husband before he was torn to shreds.

I'd been in the back of our vehicle sleeping when we were attacked. Like a coward, I pulled our travel comforter over my head and watched it happen through the space between the front seats.

There was so much gore that I'm sure it's the only reason they didn't scent a second person in the vehicle.

The horde moved on, and I cried silently for hours until he found me.

I watched him for several minutes as he decapitated the dead and scrounged for supplies in the abandoned vehicles. He was like some character in a dystopian movie. He left valuables behind and took only food and drink. The vehicle he drove had a huge tank on the back. He syphoned gas out of the cars. He was a man prepared to survive.

Unsure of whether to trust him, I vacillated back and forth between alerting him to my presence or hiding until he was gone and then striking out on my own. Until the choice was taken out of my hands. He smashed the rear window and opened the hatch.

"Who the fuck are you?" He jumped back when his gaze met mine.

"I'm the guy who just watched his husband get torn to shreds." I replied. "What were they?"

"They didn't touch you?" He tone demanded an answer.

"I was wrapped up in a blanket. I'd been asleep. They didn't know I was there."

"Probably saved your life."

I started to turn my head to the front and then shuddered. "Yes, I think you're right."

"What's your plan?" He asked.

"I have no fricken idea." I took in his appearance. He was Mad Max mixed with every lumberjack fantasy I'd ever had. "We were just coming back from a week in wine country. We've been unplugged since last Friday night. What the heck is going on?"

As we spoke, I shrugged off the big paisley comforter and shuddered at the splotches of blood all over it.

His eyes narrowed at my brightly patterned silk shirt and almond painted nails and sighed. "I can't leave you here." He looked around warily. "We've got to get moving before more of those things descend on us."

"Yes, please." I said without hesitation. "I'll get the snacks and cooler. You grab the bags and wine. We bought four cases, and I think we're going to need every last drop.

I'd been right.

Months later, we were still alive. Mostly thanks to him, my lumberjack in rustic plaid. I wish I could say I contributed but in reality, I barely qualified as the plucky sidekick.

Plucky I was not.

My twin sister and I swore we'd been gender-swapped in the womb. She was a short, stocky dynamo. Nothing phased her. She could easily wield a hammer to build a shelter whereas I was tall, slight, and my only talent was that I could plan an elegant soiree blindfolded with both hands tied behind my back.

No, I provided no advantage whatsoever. Well, except for cooking. I was a master at taking the random items we had pilfered to create something not only edible but downright delicious. Who knew there were so many ways to cook squirrel.

I wish I were joking.

He'd procured a large travel trailer, and we stored our varied provisions in the master bedroom as we wound our way into the mountains, hoping to find a safe place to spend the winter. Eventually we holed up in the barn of an abandoned house.

Both were in disrepair, but the barn provided an extra bit of camouflage and shelter against the weather and whatever was out there waiting to get us.

Whoever lived in the old house left almost everything behind. We scavenged what was usable, and I spent the winter pouring over old books of plants and herbs. Memorizing what was edible and what would kill us. There seemed to be a lot more items in the kill-us category.

As the winter wore on with both of us residing in this tiny space, I lost my sexy lumberjack fantasy real fast. Instead, I began to imagine about how pretty some of those poisonous plants would look decorating his bowl of squirrel stew.

We were two men, complete opposites, cooped up together. It did not make for a lot of harmony.

To cope, we'd fashioned a little time-out space. It was in the farthest corner of the barn, away from the trailer.

It was our place to go to have some alone time and let off steam.

So much steam that somehow, by the middle of January, we were in an unspoken contest to see who could squirt their jizz the highest up the back wall of the barn.

Neither one of us mentioned it, but each time I went out there, my cum tracks had been covered with his. Being the smart-butt I am, I brought out red and blue crayons I'd found in the house to mark the highest spray.

He had an advantage because he was almost a full head taller than me.

No, not that head. Get your mind out of the gutter. Although, if I am being completely honest, he had a rod the size of a small cannon.

I may have been smaller, but judging from the marks on the wall, just as mighty.

To help us measure the height, he provided a ladder. He also placed a big plank on the ground and labelled it "starting line" in thick black marker.

I guess I wasn't the only jokester in the building.

As winter turned into spring, we were both hornier, and crankier, than ever. Six plus months without getting laid was hard on both of us. And contrary to popular belief, just because I'm gay doesn't mean I'll fuck any male that comes along.

He's great and all, and he definitely saved my life, but that's it. Despite my little lumberjack fantasy, when I first saw him, he wasn't my type.

My husband was refined. A gentleman. We were completely devoted to each other. When we were out together in public, we never stood more than a few inches apart. It was like he was an extension of me and me of him.

My current roommate is more neanderthal than metropolitan. While he had a great ass, he'd probably tear me a new one if he ever got close to mine.

On one of the warmest days yet, he was getting on my last nerve.

We were trying to prep the soil behind the house to plant a garden. We both figured we were safer by staying here on this old homestead than trying to find our way out in the world.

I got fed up with him, not wanting to make mounds for the beans, corn and squash like one of the old books showed me. Since he was the one doing the grunt work, I gave up trying to make him listen and left him to finish the soil prep on his own and wandered off into the woods.

As I said, this happened often. So, I tried to be smart about my exploration. I'd investigate a different section each day to see what was growing and hopefully give us a better variety of food choices. I was busy trying to figure out if some berries on a huge bush were raspberries or unripe blackberries when I noticed a fresh path forged through the underbrush. It was wider than a regular deer trail, with many broken twigs and branches on the sides.

It concerned me because we were the only two people out here.

What had made such a chaotic trail?

I ran back to where he was working in the garden. "You need to see this." I told him before taking off back the way I came.

He grabbed the gun he kept handy and caught up to me in a few strides. "What did you see?"

"It looks like someone besides us is here. There's a new trail."

"Probably just animals." He said.

"You really want to take that chance?"

"Nope."

"Didn't think so." I led him to the patch of berries and pointed. "See."

His frown told me I was right to be worried.

There were deer paths all over the place, but this one seemed bigger, wider.

He stepped to the side and walked to the opening, careful not to disturb any prints in the soil. "Huh?" was all he said as he started to follow the hole in the underbrush.

"Huh? What?" I asked. Sometimes, him being such a a man of few words was annoying.

"These are all animal tracks, but they look like they're drunk. They weave back and forth for no reason."

"That's weird, right?" I'd watched deer, foxes and even a coyote walk through the field, but they'd always travelled in a reasonably straight line unless they were grazing. Then they just followed the best-looking flowers. Same with skunks and racoons too, although they were a bit more wander-y.

"Yeah, maybe they found a still or something."

"You mean like moonshine?"

"Yeah. Wouldn't that be great?" He flashed a rare smile before turning to continue on the strange trail.

Yeah. It would be. We'd finished off the last bottle of wine we'd rescued from my SUV a month ago.

I kept close, only a few steps behind him, which is why I nearly fisted him when he came to an abrupt stop.

"What the actual fuck?"

He didn't sound worried, so I stepped up beside him and I'm sure my jaw dropped to the ground.

"Those are vaginas."

He stared at me for a second.

"Don't look at me like that. I know what they look like. They're just not my preference."

We'd stopped at the edge of a clearing. In addition to the usual spring flowers, there were tall plants on broad stems that had pale pink flowers that bore an uncanny resemblance to vaginas.

He walked close to one and inhaled deeply. "They almost smell like pussies, too."

He wasn't wrong. They had a musky odour that smelled floral and feminine. "Ha, you're right."

He looked at me oddly. How would you know?

That made me laugh. "You experience a lot of smells when you're considered one-of-the-girls." I took one in my hand.

The petals were firm. At my touch, nectar seemed to pool on the surface. Releasing even more of the fragrance.

"A sea of snatch just for you. Ripe for the picking." Even though they were just flowers, I had to admit I was a little jealous. Score another one for the straight white male.

He chuckled and pointed. "Look, they made one for you."

My gaze followed his finger, and I burst out laughing. Closer to the ground grew a plant that looked like a round, juicy bubble-butt. Just the way I liked them. I fell to my knees in front of it to get a better look.

Its petals formed a tunnel with a wide, fluted edge that made it look like a small beach ball with a hole in the middle. Rather than feeling delicate, the petals stayed firm beneath my touch. Like the vagina shaped flowers, the nectar flowed as soon as I touched the petals.

I couldn't help myself, I squeezed it as if it was really a butt.

The nectar increased its volume. Droplets ran down the surface and over my fingers. The smell was intoxicating. I brought my finger to my lips to taste.

"Wait. It could be poison."

I looked at the base of the plant. All the other vegetation had been trampled into the ground by animals. "I think it's safe. This seems to be what got the deer drunk."

"You mean they were licking assholes?"

"And vaginas if the hoof prints around those plants are anything to go by," I pointed to the base of the stalk beside him and snickered. "Go ahead. See if I'm right?"

Tentatively, he reached out and touched the flower. "Damn. The petals almost feel like skin."

I cupped the butt cheek shaped flower in my hand. "They're so life-like, it's almost scary."

I glanced over when he didn't respond, to see his nose buried deep in his flower and watched him take a deep breath, his eyes almost rolled back in his head. "That stuff is a fucking aphrodisiac."

"Wow, Lumberjack. That's an awful big word." I teased.

He chuckled. The flowers obviously putting him in a much better mood than usual. "Just because I wear plaid and don't talk much, doesn't mean I'm not smart."

" Well, I never thought you were stupid. You just don't normally use multi-syllable words."

"We're stranded in the middle of butt fuck nowhere." He said. "No need for big words."

I glanced down at the flower. "Maybe we're finally in butt frick somewhere."

Following his lead, I buried my nose in the flower and took a tentative lap at the nectar directly from the source. I was already hard from the scent of the flower. The taste nearly made me cum.

I glanced back over at him, and then quickly turned away.

He'd already pulled his shaft out of his pants and was teasing the head of his cock with the outside of the flower. He wasn't self-conscious in the slightest. "You've gotta try this." His voice was tight with arousal. "The liquid from the flower intensifies every sensation. It's insane."

Now don't get me wrong, I'm all for a little bit of exhibitionism, but we'd kept to our corners so to speak all winter. It seemed weird just to suddenly let our flags fly.

But the allure of the flowers was too much. Especially combined with the soft growls coming from my roommate.

I did as he said and undid my pants and pulled myself from the waistband of my boxers. I swear the butt flower moved slightly toward me on its stem as soon as it saw my naked flesh.

Which is stupid. It's a flower, it didn't have eyes.

I ran the tip of my cock in a circle along the outer edge of the flower and then up the little crack in the middle. My eyes closed, and I had to force myself to calm down. "Holy Fuck."

I heard his laughter behind me. "Wow. Pretty-boy swore."

I ignored him. I was too focused on the sensations shooting through my body. I was on a sexual high. "What are these things?" I marvelled. Then realized I didn't care. The flowers could have come from the moon, and I'd still want to slide my cock into that narrow opening.

I was gentle at first. I didn't want to harm the flower, but it seemed to suck me in and hold me close. I drew back to push myself in again and it opened itself up, as if begging me to go deeper.

I knew it was just a flower, an inanimate object. Non-sentient.

Yet, it gripped me as I pulled out and when I pushed back in, its petals shivered. I swear the whole thing throbbed against my skin as I held still for a moment just to experience the sensation.

I could feel what must be its stamen nudging my tip. The unexpected sensation made me cum. I felt my balls tighten and the surge shooting up through my length. I tried to pull out, so I didn't damage the flower, but I just kept thrusting in and out. In and out, until I was spent.

The loud grunts beside me let me know my lumberjack had just done the exact same thing.

I'm sure later we'd both be chagrined at how fast we ejaculated into our respective blooms, even though it would be understandable since we'd both gone months with only our hands for entertainment.

Even though I'd just shot my load, my shaft was still hard, ready to go again. I held back and pulled out of the lovely little flower rump to inspect it for damage. I was worried I had hurt it.

My semen spilled out of the hole as I slid out and started to drip down over the rest of the petals. Almost immediately, it absorbed into the surface. More importantly, the flower looked no worse for wear. I glanced over at my roommate, and he was already pounding away at his blooming vagina again.

So, I did the same.

It almost felt as if the flower had been energized by absorbing my ejaculate. Then my mind went blank.

It felt so good this time I didn't hold back. I fell forward onto my hands, leaning over the flower as I thrust into it, careful not to lower my hips too far and squash it into the ground. Every thrust felt like I was harder and thicker.

The nectar from the flower was so slick yet offered the perfect level of friction. The petals seemed to tighten against me, milking me in exquisite torture.

Far too soon I felt the unstoppable rush. I was cumming again. Harder than before. My grunts and growls rivalled the lumberjacks.

When I fell back onto the earth, careful not to crush the plant, the lumberjack was already tucking himself back in his pants, but the look on his face said he wished he could go again.

I couldn't even be embarrassed at having him see my uncovered dick. I was too fatigued to care. It took me a few minutes to recover enough to get up.

My emotions were so mixed up. Guilt over enjoying sex so soon after my husband's death and wonder at the incredible flowers we'd found.

The lumberjack and I just looked at the field of flowers. Strangely, neither one of us seemed to be self-conscious about getting it off so close to each other, which was weird after our unspoken agreement to keep our self-love sessions and subsequent competition private over the course of the winter.

He was very much a straight man, and I'm sure didn't want to offer me any temptation. And, well, he just wasn't my type.

" What do we do?" I asked him. "Do you think they'd survive in the garden if we transplanted them? I bent down to take a closer look at my butt-plant... ass-alia, ass-ter. Ohh I like that. "What do you think Ass-ter? Do you want to come live in the garden near us?"

"Ass-ter?" he laughed out loud. "You're going to call it an Ass-ter."

"Sure, why not? It's not like there's anyone around to correct me."

He looked at the flower leaning contentedly against his thigh.

Who knew flowers could have personality?

"Well, if we move them and they don't survive, we have plenty more to experiment with until we get it right."

"I know, but I feel like they're more than just flowers."

He nodded as if he understood what I meant. We were their caregivers now.

"I think for now we'll keep them here." He pondered the field of plants for a moment. "I would like to try to collect some of the sap and see if we can store it."

Immediately, I knew where he was going with this. It made me laugh. The plants would most likely die in the fall, but that nectar was something special. Used as a lubricant, it could probably keep us both from going insane with only each other for company.

"That's a great idea, but I think it's important to try transporting at least a few of them closer to the house so we can observe them. Maybe even find a way to keep them growing over winter. But can we start with a flower I haven't fucked? I feel that if we're going to experiment with transplanting them into the garden, we should start with a plant I haven't had relations with. Call me silly, but I feel we should be certain before we move these particular ones."

His laugh wasn't as scornful as I was expecting. "I understand. I feel like I owe this plant to keep it as healthy as possible. I'm sure we can find a place with the same morning light as this field."

"Well, let's get back to it. We still have work to be done, and I already feel like I need a nap."

"Being gay has its advantages after all." I said with a giggle. "I was able to get on my hands and knees, you had to stand for the entire performance." I'm sure his legs felt weak as we walked back toward our encampment. "I'll search through those old books again to see if I can see any record of these plants. Although, I'm sure I would have noticed a flower like either of them."

Even though I felt like I could use a nap, I was strangely energized. If we could bottle that sap and use it, we'd be unstoppable. "Too bad the world was gone. That stuff could have made us millionaires."

The next morning armed with my gardening gloves the biggest pail I could find and a small shovel I set out for the patch of mysterious flowers. As I approached, I heard the unmistakable grunts of my lumberjack and snickered. He totally skipped his morning chores to come down to the flowers. Not that I blame him. I had done the same thing.

Still smiling, I stepped into the clearing while he was busy plunging into one of the vagina flowers again. After yesterday, all pretense of modesty vanished, at least where these plants were concerned.

Something caught my attention behind him and this time I laughed out loud. He'd brought the big washtub we'd found in the old house and the big shovel ready to transport at least one plant back to the garden. Hell, we could probably fit half a dozen stalks in that tub and between the two of us, carry it back.

I wandered over to the plant that I'd violated the day before and stroked the pinkish petals that formed its cute little rump.

They were velvety soft without tear or wrinkle. No sign of the abuse I heaped upon it the day before. In fact, it looked healthier than the rest of the plants in the field.

Who knew? Maybe my cum had a little bit of a fertilizer effect to it. Wouldn't that be something? Being forced to have amazing sex in order to properly care for these beautiful flowers.

I would absolutely do it. To keep the plants healthy, of course.

Aside from a grunted nod to acknowledge my arrival, the lumberjack continued to pound away at his flower until he howled. Jets of white coated everything in front of him with white creamy dots. When he finished, he tucked himself back in and came over to stand beside me as we decided which plants to dig up and take back to the garden.

I resisted the urge to get myself off. Starting now, after he was finished seemed too exhibitionist to me. I'd come back later once we'd done what we came to do.

We chose a couple of plants and carefully dug up around the roots. It took a while because we didn't want to damage them. As we worked, we decided to only put four in the big washtub at a time. This way we could bring along some of the dirt they were growing in to help them adapt better.

He actually laughed at me when I suggested trying to carry the tub between us. "It's safer for these beauties if you just carry the shovels."

He wasn't wrong.

He arranged the stalks so he could carry them without accidentally snapping off any of the flowers.

Once we got up to the old house, I saw that he'd already prepped the soil.

He'd dug deeply to give the root system plenty of room. I felt kind of guilty that I'd slept in this morning instead of coming out to help him. Had I known this was what he was doing, I would have been there in a heartbeat.

"Wow. Look at you go." I said, nodding to all the prep work he'd done. "I would have helped."

"It was easy for me to dig a few holes. I figured you'll be the one watering and tending to them. You're better at that stuff than me."

"Thank you." I could feel my face flush from the unexpected compliment.

Together we carefully planted the precious flowers, making sure their roots were soaked with water from the rainwater containers attached to the home's gutters.

"Should we fertilize them?" I asked the lumberjack.

"Fertilize? We already put compost in the soil."

"Didn't you notice how wonderful the flowers we fucked yesterday looked compared to the others this morning. They were practically glowing."

"I don't want to fuck them. We just transplanted them."

In a bold move, I pulled my hard rod out of my pants. "I was thinking use some of their nectar and shower them with our love."

He threw his head back and laughed. "You are so fucking corny." Still, he unzipped his jeans and stood beside me as we used the slick sap from the plants to slide our fists back and forth over our cocks, mixing our pre-cum with the nectar until we were both grunting. Fists moving furiously.

I came first. The eruption of semen coming from me exceeded any mark I'd made on the barn wall as I swivelled my hips to cover as many flowers as I could.

The sounds I made must have triggered the lumberjack. His howl echoed as he let loose. When we were done, not only the flowers were coated. Our rows of newly sprouted peas and beans were also dotted with thick cream.

I wiped the last dribble from the end of my cock and rubbed it into the closest floral ass.

The scent rising from the petals had me hard again.

Unable to resist, I dropped to my knees and plunged into its depth.

"I thought we weren't…. oh, fuck it." He said beside me and started thrusting into the nearest pussy-flower.

A week later, we had half the field transplanted. We decided to leave the rest where they were. Just to ensure we didn't inadvertently kill the ones we transplanted. Nothing in any of the gardening books mentioned these plants. So, we could only guess at their proper care, although they really, really seemed to like our cum.

We had jars of their nectar in the cellar and some on the window ledge, uncertain which way would best preserve the special qualities of the sap.

Despite our attempts to prolong the lives of the flowers, by the end of September, their stalks had turned yellow, and their petals had dried and fallen away. We gathered as many of the seeds as we could, both from our domesticated plants and those left in the meadow.

We were hoping for a bumper crop the next spring.

Fall turned to winter, and the bottled nectar in the basement stayed potent.

Not wanting any of it to go to waste, we divided the bottles and had a little hand-job festival to celebrate the harvest.

We also discovered that not only did our cum help keep the flowers vibrant, their nectar also acted like a first-aid cream. We could spread it on cuts and even bruises and they'd heal within a day or two. Even better, no matter how many times a day we jerked off, our cocks never became raw or sore.

Definitely a winning situation all around.

Amelia Dax

Melons-coly

It had been a rough year.

Dad died fighting off some thieves trying to break into our home after what-ever-the-hell happened to the world last year.

We'd come to the mountains early that spring because Mom was sick with cancer. She wanted to spend her last days in the peace and quiet of the mountains where she grew up.

Dad and I of course promised to do anything to ensure she got her final request. They sold their house and Dad and I both quit our jobs. They bought this place overlooking a lush valley, with the city beyond. If you went to the balcony on the second floor, just off from the master bedroom, you could see a glimpse of the ocean, sparkling in the distance.

We weren't completely cut off. We had satellite TV, at least until it stopped broadcasting. We knew what had happened, and how people seemed to be reanimating after they died.

Honestly, the news seemed to be something from a bad zombie movie.

To protect ourselves, Dad and I built several deterrents to prevent the mindless, diseased humans from getting to us. Unfortunately, it was no defence for fully functional people, only concerned with their own survival.

They shot Dad as soon as he approached.

They didn't see me... at all. I shot both of the intruders in the back from my spot beside the barn.

Sadly, my mom watched it all play out from her perch on the balcony. It was too much for her to take. She died a week later from a broken heart.

Before his death, Dad and I had prepared for a harsh winter. We understood it was unlikely we'd be able to go to town once the snow flew. Even less chance of that happening once the world went nuts.

The mountain retreat Mom and Dad had bought was self-sustaining. Almost everything ran on rechargeable batteries. We had solar panel arrays on the roof of the house and the garage. We'd stocked the basement with canned goods and had a cold room and several chest freezers. There was enough food to feed a small army for a year.

The food would last indefinitely, now there was only one person eating.

The winter was hard, more-so because Mom and Dad were both gone.

Spring had come, and I followed through with our survival plan. I'd planted an enormous vegetable garden, including the Brussel's sprouts my mom wanted, even though I hated them. I'd eat them with a smile and extra butter as I remembered her lectures about finishing everything on my plate.

The chickens we had brought with us were thriving and the momma goats had already given birth.

It was a far cry from my office job, but given the clouds of black smoke that had clung to the sky over the city for days, I assumed there was not an office left to return to.

I was living the life of a dystopian novel. Except for the solitude, I kind of liked it.

With my pistol in my hand and knife tucked into its sheath on my belt, I walked the path we'd cut around our home with various decoy off-shoots, to take unexpected guests back down the mountain instead of toward our home.

The main path was far enough away from our house that a stranger could follow it and never see the buildings. I walked it every few days to see if anyone besides an animal had been near. It was seriously brilliant.

Who knew my dad had advanced survival skills?

Ever vigilant, I watched for movement, but also looked for plants to eat until my garden yielded more than radishes and spinach. I was almost ready to turn back when out of the corner of my eye I saw a large pinkish flower a few meters from the path.

It hadn't been there yesterday when I'd walked this same section.

Curiously, I approached. The bloom wasn't like anything I'd seen before. Not that I was a botany expert or anything, but I would have remembered this.

As I approached, a sweet, musky scent surrounded me. It was familiar even though I couldn't place it.

My dick stirred in my pants. That's weird, I thought, until I got closer to the plant and realized the flower looked like a perky boob atop of a sturdy stalk.

I chuckled. No wonder I got a chubby.

Not that I believed in all that woo-woo crap, but this had been a weird year, and it would be just like my dad to send a message like this to say everything would be okay.

He knew I was a breast man, just like him.

"C'mon Dad." I said aloud to the woods. "Just one?"

The clouds shifted in the sky as if moving the sun's spotlight through the treetops to a small clearing filled with these strange flowers. Some were single, some bloomed in pairs, and a few had groups of three reaching for the sun from a single thick stem.

This made me laugh out loud. These were definitely sent by my father. There was absolutely no doubt about it.

When I was barely sixteen, Mom snooped in my room because a friend of mine had been caught with dope.

She panicked and searched my room to ease her mind. Instead of drugs, she found a sci-fi, alien porn graphic novel. She took it to Dad and told him to handle it.

Dad of course, read it from cover to cover, twice, or so he told me years later, before taking me outside to the garage to have a 'talk'. Which consisted of making sure I had realistic expectations of relationships and to show me a better place to hide my stash from my mother.

He loved the aliens with three boobs. Hell, he bought me the rest of the series so we could both enjoy them... separately, of course.

I looked up at the sky. "Thanks Dad." Then, as an afterthought, I added. "Don't worry, I won't tell Mom."

Cautiously, I examined the flowers.

The petals extended out from the end of their stems to form a wide ball nearly the size of my fist. Instead of flaring out like flowers normally do, they drew themselves back to a single point, then a small burst of secondary petals extended out by a centimeter. They looked firm, but I was hesitant to touch it with my bare hand.

I had no way of knowing if the nectar was poison.

Just then, a squirrel started chittering at me from the trees a few meters away. Its tail twitched with agitation as it glared at me. It raced up and down the tree and then kept up its barrage. Finally, after my stillness seemed to convince it I wasn't a threat, it scurried to the ground and up the stalk of one of the boob plants. Then it gripped the fat bloom in its tiny paws and extended its body backwards to be able to lick at the tiny petals at the end.

Seriously, I've seen squirrels have sex, and this was far more erotic. The squirrel wasn't eating the petals, just lapping up the moisture, in complete blissed-out joy.

Judging by its protectiveness of this treat, it wasn't the first time he'd sampled the sweet.

I have to admit, the smell was intoxicating. I paused, trying to figure out what it reminded me of. Then it hit me. There was an underlying layer of musk. It smelled like walking into a room after someone had just had sex.

Since I was already on my knees to get a better look at the flower, I reached out with the tip of my finger to trace along the variegated pink veins in the petals. They felt velvety. If I closed my eyes, I could easily mistake them for soft skin.

As soon as I touched the flower, nectar beaded at the tip. Right in the center of the circle of small petals.

"Huh, so that's what you're drinking." I said to the squirrel, who was still intently focused on the flower between his grabby paws.

I touched my finger to the center and rubbed the silky liquid between my fingers. My skin tingled. I brought my hand to my face and the intense smell sent a jolt through my body. To my surprise, the heady fragrance made my chubby harden into a full-blown erection. I looked down in surprise to see my cock straining against the fabric of my jeans.

Fuck, no wonder that squirrel was protective.

Without giving myself a chance to talk myself out of it, I licked the residue from the pad of my finger and groaned. So good.

I held the round bloom between my palms and squeezed it gently. It was firmer than I expected. Its surface squishing slightly when I applied pressure, but it bounced back to its original shape when I let go.

Just like a real tit.

More sap eased out from the tiny ring of petals and dribbled down over the flower's round surface.

This time, I licked the drops directly from the petals. A shudder ran through my body and settled in my balls. I felt an irresistible urge to jerk off.

Uncaring about how vulnerable I'd be if I shifted my attention from my surroundings, I undid my belt and pulled my cock out.

The plant's sap on my hand was slick against my hard shaft when I gripped it, trying to stave off the orgasm. The tingling sensation from the sap had me ready to cum almost immediately. I'd never been so hard in my life.

Two strokes later, and I was done.

White dots blanketed the flower and its neighbours.

I felt guilty for making such a mess, but then, to my shock, my jizz disappeared like water into the soil. Completely absorbed by the greenery.

I should probably have been alarmed but couldn't rouse the concern.

My dick hadn't softened in the slightest. The urge to cum again was overwhelming as I jerked my cock, occasionally adding more nectar from the flower as a lubricant. It mixed with the steady stream of pre-cum sliding out from the tip of my dick. The stimulation with every stroke of my hand was life altering. Every nerve ending was on fire in the best possible way, as I gripped my cock.

I came three times.

The last time I was ramming my cock head directly at the ring of petals where the liquid magic came from. I was long past worrying about damaging the flower in my quest for the next powerful orgasm.

After the last time, my skin felt raw from the friction and the tightness of my grip.

As if sensing my changing needs, the nectar became soothing. It cooled my overheated skin, and the tingles felt refreshing instead of arousing.

Spent, I dropped to the side, pants still bunched around my knees.

If anyone approached, I was a sitting duck, and I didn't give a flying fuck.

It took a while to recover. It had been almost two years since I'd had sex, and I don't think I'd ever cum so many times in a row.

When mom made her decision to stop treatments, my girlfriend of six months refused to move to the mountains with us. A city-girl through and through, she thought I was nuts for giving up everything to fulfil my mother's last request. It's not that she was a bad person. She'd grown up in foster homes and couldn't imagine giving up her hard-won security for anyone.

We promised to keep in touch and maybe reunite after Mom passed, if she hadn't already moved on.

It's kind of ironic that now I'm the one with any sort of existence. I doubted she was still alive after the devastation in the cities.

Rather than go down that rabbit hole of sorrow, I turned my attention back to the flower with aphrodisiacal properties.

It didn't look any different now than before I rammed my cock against its bloom. The petals weren't bruised.

Curious, I pulled the knife from my belt. I wanted to see what the flower was made of.

To my surprise, I felt a slight tug along the palm of my hand as the bloom seemed to drag itself away from me.

The rest of the flowers did the same until the entire grove angled themselves away from where I sat. It was unnatural. They should have been stretching toward the sun, which was in the sky behind me. The scent changed, too. It soured until it smelled like vomit.

I stood, nearly falling flat on my face because of the forgotten denim still circling my calves.

I dropped the knife and pulled my pants up. When I reached down to retrieve my blade, it was half buried by the plant's roots.

It freaked me the fuck out.

I pulled the knife from the earth, careful to avoid the roots that parted slowly to give me access.

Almost as if it was trusting me to do the right thing.

I'm not sure why, but I sheathed the blade again.

The entire flower patch seemed to droop in relief.

I reached out to cup my palm around the blossom. "I'm sorry. I won't harm you."

The petals seemed to relax into my hand. Much like a puppy begging for an ear scratch.

I stroked along the petals with my finger. Amused that I felt the need to soothe it.

The surrounding air changed again. Sweeter than before, and even though I'd already cum three times in quick succession, my horny cock was rising again.

I couldn't resist the temptation. I stepped over to the triple blooms and this time I toed off my boots and tugged my jeans from my legs and kicked them aside. Since I'm not an idiot, I put my boots back on.

I'm sure I looked a sight, but honestly, if someone tried to attack me now, seeing a half-naked man running after them is probably more terrifying than someone fully clothed.

And, if my past girlfriends were to be believed, the gun swinging between my legs was intimidating enough on its own.

Not to this mysterious plant, though. Its three blooms were already stretching toward me on their stalk, angling the flowers up as if hoping I'd slide my cock in the narrow gaps between them. It was as if it had read the same graphic novels I had as a teen.

Eager to see if it would work, I held the outer two blooms close to the center one and slid my cock under their globes. Coating my skin with the silky fluid dripping freely from their petal-like nipples.

It was electric. The sensations radiated out from my cock through my torso until I felt like I was going to pass out from the pleasure. My toes curled inside my boots to help keep me upright as my knees threatened to buckle.

I pulled back slightly to manoeuvre my dick on top of the melon like flowers. The feel of those tiny petals as they rubbed the underside of my shaft and teased at my balls nearly sent me into orbit. Without thinking, I stabbed the spaces in between their stems. Instead of being rough or prickly, they were as soft as the petals, except they had a slightly ridged texture that made every thrust better than the last.

Ribbed for her pleasure, my ass.

Soon I got into a rhythm of plunging myself into one gap, dragging the tip of my cock along the bottom of the flower to pick up more of the nectar, before thrusting into the other.

Ho-ly Fuck.

I was a machine, driving myself in and out between the gaps. Each one felt different than the other, as if I was fucking two women at once. A tight virgin and a set of plump pussy lips that suctioned the head of my cock every time I pulled out. Even the stalk played a part. As I entered the gap, I hit the thick stem and slid up its girth. Its grooved texture acted like another wall to hug my dick as it moved in and out.

The nectar kept the perfect balance between slick and friction.

Better than my wildest fantasies about fucking a three-breasted alien.

My legs were ready to give out by the time my balls drew up. I was exhausted but couldn't bear to stop. Just a few more strokes and I knew I was going to have the orgasm to end all orgasms.

The explosion from my sac took me out at the knees. I landed on my back and dry humped the air as shot after shot of cum arced over the flowers, their stems, and my thighs.

Finally, my cock seemed to heave against my leg with nothing left to give.

I lay there long enough to watch the sun move across the sky.

Like before, the flowers absorbed my spunk. The lower leaves even seemed to drape over my junk to clean up where I'd spurted across my leg, then they remained to protect me from sunburning my bits.

Now that I was coming back to myself, I had to fight the urge to say, "Thank you." It slipped out anyway as I rolled over onto my knees and pushed myself up.

After a quick look around to make sure I was still alone, I put my pants back on. It took three tries to do up the button because my handshaking so much. Fatigue was starting to set in. I needed a nap.

I looked at the enclave of flowers and wondered what I could do to move them closer to the house. Would they transplant well or would I have to wait until fall and gather the seeds. There was no question. I needed more of these plants if I was going to survive life alone.

They were the closest thing I'd had to human contact in almost a year.

When I got home, I took a shower. While the nectar felt good in the moment, I realized how foolhardy my little sexual adventure had been. I carefully examined myself for splinters or thorns and was surprised to see that the skin that I'd rubbed raw was already healed.

The sap seemed to be a salve as well as an aphrodisiac.

Way better than my mother's aloe vera plant.

I needed that plant in my house for the winter. For so many reasons.

The next day I took some time to prepare a new spot in my garden. It mimicked the flower patch for sun exposure. I had to give the boob-like flowers a name, boob-bells, titty-tails… in the end, I decided to just call them melons.

I had to give the melons the best chance of survival.

Then I took my shovel, three large buckets, and the little garden wagon my mom had used to the clearing. This way, I didn't have to carry the large plants uphill all the way back to the house.

The plants drifted in my direction on their stems as I approached. Oddly enough, three stalks seemed to have separated themselves. They stood a few feet in front of the others, as if offering themselves as tribute.

As if they knew I would want to take them home with me today.

The thought freaked me out, but after yesterday's experience, I was going to do everything in my power to ensure I didn't have to spend a day without my new friends.

Gently, I cleared away the ground around the stalks, trying to get a sense about how far out the roots grew, so I didn't accidentally nick them with my shovel. I wanted to give them the best chance of survival.

Glad I had remembered the garden trowel, I pulled it from my back pocket and started to dig a few inches past where I thought the roots would extend.

The ground was looser than I expected, so the going was easy and after I dug a trench around the first plant, I switched to my hands and then just dug with my fingers. Surprisingly, instead of reaching out like most roots, these curled back on themselves into a root ball as if they'd already prepared themselves for transplant.

I grinned up at the flower with words of praise for making this project so easy. I was only mildly surprised when there wasn't a face looking back at me. I'd already become used to thinking of them as sentient instead of just titties on a stick.

Carefully, I put the first bucket in the wagon. The second two plants were that much easier to uproot because I knew what I was doing.

I filled the rest of the wagon with the same soil from around the plants to prevent the shock of being planted in different soil up in the garden.

Once I got them up to the house, I was reluctant to put them in the ground with the beans, carrots and, of course, Mom's Brussels sprouts.

Instead, I looked long and hard at the glassed-in porch on the sunny side of the house.

It seemed a little disrespectful to put sexual play toys in the room where mom spent many of her last few months before she was put on bedrest.

Part of me wondered if they'd bloom all year if I sheltered them inside.

I consoled myself with knowing Mom wanted me to find someone. Neither of us could have foreseen the way the world had gone to shit and how few options for company I had.

I watered the plants but kept them in the wagon while I searched through the garage for something to make a permanent flower bed inside the house.

Two hours later, I had a large, claw-footed bathtub set up in the sunroom with a drainage pan underneath to catch any excess water. All three plants were nestled in the earth. The tub had enough space that I didn't have to crowd them all together. I'd taken another quick run down to the clearing and brought back a second wagon full of dirt to ensure they had enough soil to thrive.

I was hesitant, but I put a little bit of fertilizer in with the water as I gave them a good soaking. I didn't want to put too much in until I knew how they'd react to something commercially made.

That night I pulled over one of the comfy chairs and sat beside the tub naked from the waist down, even though I had no intention of fucking the flowers.

Transplanting was a shock to a plant's system, and they'd been through a lot today.

While I didn't want to harm them, I still fondled their roundness and gathered the nectar from their nipple-like petals and rubbed it along my cock until it was slick with their juices.

I gave myself lazy strokes as my other hand caressed each melon, letting their weight settle in my palm and brushed my thumb over the tiny petals at their tip, moving from one to the other, making sure they all got equal attention.

All too soon, my grip on my cock got harder as I jerked my fist back and forth along its slick surface. Soon just moving my hand wasn't enough, and I started thrusting my hips up to meet my fist until I came so hard my gasp echoed around the room. My spunk scattered all over the plants and their stalks.

It seemed the more I came, the faster they drank me in.

That field of flowers chose well when they decided which of them would come live in my house with me. The chosen were very healthy plants and as a bonus that I appreciated more and more every day, they gave me a single, a double, and a triple. A pretty trifecta, with stalks flexible enough to be used in so many different positions to satisfy a man's every fantasy.

Trust me, I had plans for that single boob-like flower. I'd circle that puppy with the tip of my cock like a winning number. Letting its juicy goodness spread all over my flesh until we both vibrated with need. Or nurse from it while fucking between the triple melons.

Summer passed in a horny frenzy.

I'd get up and spend time with my plants before heading out for the day. Cumming so hard should have worn me out, but it energized me instead.

I stopped bothering to make coffee the week after I brought those little melons from heaven into my home.

After getting the outside tasks done, I'd head down to the patch where the rest of the plants were preparing for autumn. The colder nights were already affecting their firmness, and I could see the telltale traces of yellow creeping up their stalks.

Even though they were drooping, I fucked the wild melons with the same ferociousness as the ones in my home. There was something extra special in the way their softer texture cradled my dick between them. I didn't have to limit myself to just thrusting in the gaps between their stems as I did in the spring.

Who knew sagging tits could be even more arousing than the perky ones? It was a fun lesson to learn.

The blooms in my house were starting to droop too. It seemed moving them inside gave them only a life extension. They were starting to yellow at the base of their stems where they attached to the stalk.

I thought I had only days left until they were gone.

A week passed and, to my surprise, at the base of their stalks, new sprouts started to grow.

I added a little more fertilizer, and to be truthful I may have aimed a few orgasms in the sprout's direction as well.

They thickened up in no time.

While I nurtured the new life growing in my home, I came to see the outdoor melons for what I could only assume to be the last time.

They glistened in the sunlight. Their rosy hue paler and petals drying out at the edges giving them a ruffled look. A vast difference from the day before.

I stroked them softly while digging my cock out of my pants.

I had planned just to jerk off as I touched them since their sweet nectar had all but dried up since it got colder.

But the blooms seemed to have a plan of their own.

As I rubbed each one, it loosened from its stem and fell into my hand. They'd shrunk enough that two or three could fit in each palm.

Since there was no way to save them, I held them together and thrust into the little melons made of petals and let my hips take over the action.

It was like fucking a slice of heaven right there in the palm of my hands. The soft firmness, still warm from the sun and slick from their combined nectar, felt even more like a woman's cunt than ever before.

I used the crushed petals to wipe up the cum and realized there were seeds inside the broken fibres of the flowers.

I carefully wiped my hands on my shirt, keeping the seeds in one spot so I could wrap them safely to take them back to my house.

The next spring, I still planted enough vegetables to get me through the year, but half the garden was filled with these wonderful flowers.

Sorry Mom, no room for Brussel's sprouts.

Epilogue

It was June, and she was barely able to tend to her garden. Her stomach was so round with the child that had been conceived after a hedonistic summer with Mr. Prickles.

In a moment of whimsy, she'd changed his name from just Prickles once she found out she was pregnant. It seemed less dirty that way. Not that there was anyone around to judge.

She rubbed over a protruding limb that kept poking out from her belly. "Soon, Darlin'" she crooned. "Soon."

She tried not to think about what was growing in her body. Plants didn't just randomly impregnate people. She had to believe there was a greater plan at work here than just a horny summer spent humping a flower.

She was a logical person, so she had everything ready; water, towels, baby clothes, and a machete… just in case. She hadn't seen another human over the winter and hoped like hell one didn't show up when she was this vulnerable.

The plants that had grown in her pot since March bent toward her when she entered her dwelling. It was as if they knew her time was close.

Sure enough, within the hour, she was trying to muffle her screams each time she felt the urge to push.

Later, with a baby girl nursing at her breast, she sat on her bed beside Mr. Prickle's offspring. They reverently touched the baby's head.

As she watched her little miracle fall asleep, she could see the faint veins in the baby's cheeks, just like petals.

She let herself heal for a few weeks, religiously rubbing in the nectar from the penis plants into her skin, as she'd found it to be a wonderfully soothing salve.

Until the day the plants must have sensed she'd healed enough.

Instead of calming her nerves after a late night with a crying baby, the cream from the tips of her penis crop created a new, yet familiar hunger.

While the babe finally slept, she raised her sleep dress and bent over, pushing her ass toward the three closest pink mushroom-headed shafts. Two slowly stroked her ass as the third one drooped enough to lean into her channel.

She reached between her legs to guide it in, then slide it out and in again.

The ridge around its head was exquisite as it rubbed back and forth along her g-spot.

Gasping, she moved the flower cock faster. "Fuck, it's been so long." She whispered into the quiet room, eying her daughter, hoping she stayed asleep.

This crop of penis plants had more flexibility and movement than the original Mr. Prickles. They were more lifelike in so many ways.

Now two of them plunged into her depths.

She stifled a scream as the third one somehow ducked under and between her legs. Its tip rubbed against her clit, which sent a new set of sensations skittering across her spine.

Every time she pushed back against them, they pushed forward, rubbing her inside and out with precision until she was drenched.

Her juices mixed with theirs.

With one final push against them, she rubbed herself against their bases. Their leaves adding to the friction and pressure she desperately needed. Panting for relief, she came. Soaked with arousal she leaned forward on her forearms. Surprised that her babe slept through her scream at the end.

Meanwhile, the plants behind her started the task of cleaning her up. Absorbing her juices along with their nectar.

As she rolled over to fall asleep on her cot, her last thought was an image of her daughter and other hybrid children playing in the fields. Immune to those damn diseases.

Afterword

If you enjoyed this story, please leave a review on Goodreads or your favourite book retailer. Your reviews help more than you can imagine.

Stay Sexy,
Amelia

Other Books by Amelia Dax

Earth Outpost 6-9

Nestled near the asteroid belt between Mars and Jupiter, Earth has 360 monitoring stations. Damian and Elin are stationed at Outpost 6-9. A coincidence? Perhaps not. They will do anything to make their interstellar guests feel welcome… ANYTHING.

Language Specialist Dax and Inter-Cultural Expert / Empath Amelia are kindred spirits. They roam their outpost monitoring station without clothes, eager to do whatever it takes to make their interstellar guests feel welcome.

Eventually, they learn their role isn't just fun and games. The universe is vast, humans are weak, and soon they'll need all the interstellar friends they can get.

If you enjoy fun, sexy-times, you'll love this short story series.

Author Bio

Forgettable by day and incredible at night, Amelia Dax takes inspiration from the world around us she crafts stories of lust and satisfaction.